DISCIPLE OF THE UNDEAD

ISABELLE DRAKE

For more information contact:
Riverdale Avenue Books
Afraid Imprint
5676 Riverdale Avenue
Riverdale, NY 10471

www.riverdaleavebooks.com

Design by www.formatting4U.com
Cover by Scott Carpenter

Digital ISBN: 9781626016415
Print ISBN: 9781626016422

First Edition October 2022

Dedication
For Treachery.
Now that I have seen you, you are no longer hidden.

Chapter One
"I'm not hard to find."

Monday night and still at work, Hayden Buchanan Thomas sorted paper clippings and article printouts his boss, Elizabeth Hume, had left on his desk. This was not the distinguished newspaper position he'd dreamt about and hustled for. Some of the pieces in the pile were bullshit he'd written a couple months ago for Bob Keeler's ridiculous but influential tabloid, *The Boston Weekly*. Some were articles he'd written for *The Globe*, his current paper of employment. Both sets were cold accounts of the zombie tribe that had recently infected Boston. The myth he'd created was that the creatures had arrived in a blizzard and stayed, crawling closer and deeper into the city with each wintery day. Everything he'd written—zombies roaming the streets, capturing humans, using the captives as sex slaves, using the humans' sexual energy as sustenance—came across as the usual exaggerated tabloid crap. But it was all true. Still true. Unbelievably disgusting, truly terrifying, but true. He knew that because he'd lived it. And was still living it. And would continue living it until he found a way to get free.

The rest of the pages, the ones he had not written, were pieces from local websites, personal blogs, and even a couple from the *Boston Herald*. Each of those made a reference to one or more of the vacant, dilapidated buildings around town.

His task for the evening was to combine the two sets of information. To figure out how, in reality or in his imagination, the Tribe of the Undead was making use of the empty buildings. As a first step in accomplishing that, he'd been asked to make a list of all the vacant buildings and code them by location and condition. Also, create some sort of "coolness" scale and use that scale to rate the decrepit, crumbling places. And, of course, note which of the locations were most likely to be possessed by evil entities. That last bit was key. The result being a top five list of the "coolest," most likely to be haunted ruins in Beantown. The second step, connecting the tribe of sex-cult zombies to the battered and forgotten buildings, had yet to be revealed.

He turned to the plain window centered on the small, plain wall of the plain room. Outside, the gray March clouds hung low, smothering the setting sun. The limbs of the trees shook from the wind, the bare branches poking at the sky like bony fingers. He'd felt the chill of the day all afternoon even though he'd been right there for hours. The indoor space was as grim as the sky. They all referred to the room as a cooperative collaboration space, but it was in actuality a shitty room they were all forced to share because in actuality the well-respected *Globe* newspaper did not admit to them or their work. With the exception of their uncompromising, well-connected leader, Elizabeth Hume, the paper acknowledged none of them individually or them as a whole. They were the newspaper's money-making secret. The secret was so tightly kept, that not everyone who worked in this obscure end of the building knew that they were involved in something so ridiculous.

Sure, a few of them occasionally got some credit for something that made its way onto the paper's actual website, but on the whole, he knew that the paper did not want the public to know what went on in that room.

Months ago, when his whole purpose in life was to get an actual job at an actual paper where he'd begin his actual career, Hayden would have been okay with working late to get what he wanted. The idea was that respectable employment would give him the money he needed to pay his student loans while also stopping him from being the laughingstock of his graduate program. Sure, he'd achieved one of those goals, getting paid, but ironically that money came with a hefty price tag. One that he was still paying and would still be paying long after that last loan payment cleared his bank.

"That one of the top-secret projects Hume has you working on?"

Hayden turned to find Nidhi Bansal leaning into the doorway. Elizabeth's glorified errand girl was one of the people who didn't fully understand what really went on in the office. Covered by her long gray overcoat and with her ever-present brown leather messenger bag over her shoulder, she was obviously done for the day. He waved his hands over the papers. "Yes, and see how grand it is? Do try to hold back your jealousy."

She laughed, but the sound didn't ring true. "I'm the one on my way out the door while you're the one stuck here doing this busy work. I don't think that's cause for jealousy."

Nidhi's constant curiosity over his projects was something Hayden had adjusted to from his first day on the job. Him working there had been the result of a favor, one Bob Keeler owed him, but she had no way of knowing that. So, he'd been vague in his reply and assumed she'd give up on her queries. He'd been wrong. She constantly asked him what he was working on and why he was the one assigned to it. Her questions got honest, yet ambiguous, answers. It seemed she thought he was a threat to her own employment, but that was not the case. Not at all. And he never would be. This position was temporary for him. It had to be. And so, he was just passing through. Edging, like everyone else who knew what they were up to, for a successful, upward, exit.

He chuckled and did his best to look sheepish. The expression usually worked with women, but apparently not her. "You are the lucky one tonight," he said, turning back to the papers and hoping she'd offer a quick goodnight and leave.

Instead, she spoke again. "By the way, I'm not the only one asking about you."

He replied without looking up. "Hume?"

"Nope. Both she and Darrel left."

He took the bait and lifted his head. Something curious lingered in her eyes. If he knew her better, he could be certain, but to him it looked like excitement. Thanks to the recent turns in his life, he had to be on guard constantly. He'd learned to trust his intuition and see everything, and everyone, as a threat. And so, the sick sensation swelling in his gut was not pointless anxiety. It was a clear warning.

When she continued, her lips curled into a discerning grin. "A girl in the bathroom. She asked if you were around. Seems she's looking for you."

"Who…" But, of course, he already knew who it was, loitering in the bathroom, lingering until everyone except him left this part of the building.

"Not my business to ask her name," she said. Still grinning, she continued, "She looks…"

He lifted his eyebrows, knowing exactly how she probably looked but stayed silent, not wanting to give Nidhi the satisfaction of hearing him speak the words aloud.

Her gaze lingered on him for a while. Finally, apparently accepting that he was not going to offer a description, she said, "Expensive. In a paid for kind of way."

Nidhi Bansal had no idea just how paid for that girl was. "Well." He lifted then dropped his hands onto the sea of white paper spread across the desk. The dramatic thump did nothing to ease the tension seizing his guts. He feigned a light tone, "I'm not hard to find."

"Oh, but you are."

Mattie, now behind Nidhi.

Directly behind.

Close enough that she was pressing her massive tits against the other girl's back. So close she could easily grind her crotch into Nidhi's ass. She lifted her arms and braced herself in the doorway, spread her booted feet, and hung like a spider; Nidhi tucked into her web. A red flush burst across Nidhi's cheeks, spread across her face, crept down her neck. Eyes wide, mouth trembling, she stepped into the room, walked over to stand in front of the window, and said, "I see you did find him."

Embarrassment? Excitement? Hayden couldn't tell what emotion was making Nidhi flutter.

"Guess I'll get going," she added but made no effort to leave.

Mattie didn't move either. She tilted her head, the messy bun of her tangled hair dropped to the side. A faint mocking smile played across her lips. Lips that had been everywhere on Hayden's body. Lips that had made him do and say things he never would've imagined possible. Those things and more. All possible. All real. And now all a part of who and what he was. Who and what he would always be. Hayden didn't want his co-worker brought into this fucked up, humiliating part of his life. "Get out of her way."

"Am I bothering you?" Mattie asked, leering at the other girl, her gaze a savage assessment of Nidhi's body. Hayden had never seen Mattie smile the way she was now. Wanton. Coy. Envious. With her leather jacket zipped up, hiding her huge tits, and her powerful thighs covered by plain jeans, she almost looked human. Almost. But not to him. He knew who—what—she was and that her manipulative extremes were as formidable as they were endless.

Judging by the softened and sexy expression on Nidhi's face, Mattie's smile ignited the girl's imagination and her lust. Not at all surprising. The creature had snared him in a similar, if more aggressive, way.

Nidhi shook her head. "Bothering isn't the word I'd use. I—"

Hayden masked his angst with irritation. "Nidhi was on her way out. Please get out of the doorway, so she can go home."

"Nidhi. I like the way that sounds. I'd like to say it more. But fine, have it your way, Hayden. You do like to ruin everyone's fun." Mattie relinquished the doorway by dropping her arms and moving slightly into the room.

Nidhi paused, then hopped forward, casting the girl a sideways glance as she passed into the outer office. Seconds later the snap of the lobby door confirmed her exit.

Mattie moved back to close the door with an exaggerated softness. "It's just you and me now."

Hayden leaned forward, bracing himself for the icy flow of heat she elicited. "What do you want?"

Peering at the papers and notes scattered around, she came closer. "Working on the possession project I see."

He shoved the pages into a pile, slid the stack away from her then leaned back to set his feet on the edge of the desk.

"I had a nice chat with your friend, Nidhi."

Hayden tried to ignore the obviously sexual way she pronounced the other girl's name. "We aren't friends. We're co-workers."

"Has she told you about her research project?"

He kept his mouth closed as he folded his arms.

"She gave me an earful. Told me some secrets, I think." She pulled her bottom lip inward and bit down, making the flesh pucker, then spoke again. She knows more than you think. More than she should."

Doubtful. Very doubtful. "She talked Hume into letting her work on Tribexx stuff," he said. "I think she's working on some posts about clothes, music, and culture."

"Culture. That sounds intriguing." She faked a pout. "I have to admit though, I don't like being reduced to a fandom."

"You aren't the fandom."

"So true." She lifted her eyebrows and turned her head to the side, staring down at him. "I'm the real thing. Makes me special, don't you think?"

Hayden smirked. "You going to offer to do an interview?"

"Nah," she replied, stretching out the word and

parting her lips. "I know how you reporters love the quest for knowledge. I wouldn't want to make her hunt too easy." She wiggled her fingers and then pointed at him. "You need to keep an eye on her. Make sure she doesn't get herself into something she isn't ready for."

Bitter electricity ignited his nerves. The chair squeaked when he eased it back even further. "Don't tell me what to do."

She knocked his legs from the desk. His feet hit the floor with a hard thud. "That ring doesn't change everything," she said, placing herself on the edge of the desk, looming above him.

As he often did, he looked at the crest on the gold pinky ring he was still getting accustomed to wearing. "It changes some things."

"What things?" She put her booted feet on his thighs, pressed down, spreading his legs apart. "I'm not seeing, or feeling, anything different right now."

The words rang true, but he clung to his new vision of his reality. The two of them weren't going back to how things had been. Never. "I'm not your pet anymore." Pleasure and pain mingled. "That's one thing that's different."

"True." She continued pressing, grinding her heels into his thighs. "You're Lizzie's puppet. Aren't you?"

There was no disputing that. The scattered papers now shuffled into a pile were the evidence her bidding was his call. No matter how stupid the task, he was her go to boy. Trapped here in this odd section of the building, an office separated from the rest of the staff, the real writers and reporters. This little corner belonged to Elizabeth Hume alone and alone she decided what to do with her resources. He was nothing more than a resource.

"Seems you are catching on."

He gave in and asked, "To what?"

"That your entire world is on a need-to-know basis."

"Is that why you're here?" Pulling away from her would be a sign of weakness, so he resisted the urge. "I need to know something?"

She reached for the zipper tab on her leather, started gliding it down, exposing a tight black T-shirt beneath. Once the zipper was all the way open, she arched her back and let the jacket slide to her elbows. She shook her arms. The jacket landed on the table, covering half of the pile of articles. "Maybe you do. Maybe you don't."

"Seems to me I do."

"Don't be such an asshole Hayden." She eased up on his thighs, moved one foot to his crotch. "Why don't you ever like to have fun anymore?"

The light pressure against his dick was a threat, he knew. Do what I want, say what I want, or I'll hurt you. He'd played this game with her enough times to know he was going to lose. He always lost. Still, he grabbed her foot with both hands and twisted outward, forcing her to lift and straighten her leg, while she moved it away from him. She placed the other foot on his crotch, this time pressing harder. Hard enough to hurt. Again, he reached for her foot with both hands and again she kicked her leg outward and away from him. This time though, she lunged forward, knocking him and the chair to the ground. There wasn't much of a struggle. She grabbed him, pulled him from the chair and then crawled on top of him, pinning him to the floor with her hands and knees.

He would have been happier with himself if he had the urge to fight or at least get angry, but those emotions were long gone. Instead, he felt his body respond to her bitter scent, her overwhelming strength, and her cold hunger for him. In the past she had come to him, used him, because she needed him. Now, though, she came to him because she wanted him, and she knew that in the obscure dreadful place in his soul, he wanted her too.

"If I let go of you, are you going to be a good boy and unzip your pants for me?"

He clenched his jaw, felt the saliva surge in the back of his mouth.

She threw her head back and laughed, a cruel mirth that made his chest heave. But still, he reached down and unzipped his pants, shoved the fabric down.

"And?" she mocked.

He shoved his boxers down.

"That's more like it, puppet."

She got off him long enough to pull down her own jeans, leaving them around her ankles, bunched above her boots. "Why are you looking at me like that? Did you have some stupid idea I'd turned into a decent girl and start wearing panties?"

He lay there, hand on his dick, in the middle of the collaborative space. The chair lay sideways next to him, unfinished work on the desk. He waited, wanting, needing her to drop herself on top of him. Fuck him. Release the grim ugliness that had settled inside him. Instead of lowering herself onto his cock, she folded her arms under her tits and glared at him.

"I like seeing you on your back, like that. Reminds me of your first visit to the camp."

He let go of his cock and grabbed her leg, squeezed hard, wanting his nails to scratch her flesh. "I don't give a shit what you like."

The sky had grown more bleak, the black tips of the

trees just visible in the corner of the window dotted the sky. Grim, but a reminder that elsewhere normal people lived their normal lives.

"I think when I tell you that thing you need to know, you're going to start caring about what I like."

"Tell me now and find out," he said, continuing to squeeze even though he knew he couldn't hurt her.

"As I just told you, I like seeing you this way. I'm enjoying myself, Hayden. It's called having fun." She put her hand between her legs and caressed her bare pussy. "You should try it sometime."

He pulled on her leg, but the pressure he applied did nothing to knock her off balance. Still stroking herself, she stood above him, the mocking smile he knew so well pulling on her mouth. Beaten for now, he closed his eyes, moved his hand back to his cock and began rubbing, letting himself step into her cruel realm. One day he would get away from her and her depraved world. For now, he understood that the only way to get out was to go all the way in, hunt down her weakness, the weakness for all of them, then use it against them. Break them. Or at least break their tie to him. He wrapped his other hand around his shaft, the pinky ring cutting into his skin, reminding him how tied he was.

As though she was inside his mind, feeling his despair, she laughed. He took his hands away, opened his eyes. She was staring at him, the cruel gleam in her eyes familiar and haunting. Keeping his gaze locked with her own, she put one knee on each side of his body. The pants still clustered around her calves limited her movement as she squatted over him, making her wobble. She grabbed the edge of the desk, then worked her body into position and finally began covering his cock with her tight, cold pussy. Poison flowed through him, igniting his need to be inside her, feel her take him.

Use him.

Inch by inch she worked herself down, until finally he felt the cool brush of her ass against him. He straightened his legs, pressed them together as he thrust up, driving his cock into her. The familiar plunge was, as always, both relieving and revolting. Over the past months he had come to know that no matter how sickening and shocking the sexual trip he took with her, he would come back to himself on the other side. The excruciating perfection of their coupling had become a necessary evil for him, something to silence the demons his time with the tribe had awakened. But only for now, not forever, he promised himself—again—as he gave himself permission to accept the dreadful condition.

He used his heels as a level to lift himself higher and drive his cock in, but soon her weight took the strength from his body. He had no choice but to lie there and allow her to fuck him. He opened his eyes, forced himself to watch her. Again and again, she ground into him, hardly moving her hips as she overpowered him.

"Yes, puppet," she said, clutching the desk with one hand and his shoulder with the other. "Right now, I'm your master."

The hideous physical pleasure remained, tormenting him with his own hunger. Coils of need and desire rose, wrapped themselves around him. His nerve endings were on fire, his mind blown. She increased her speed, driving up and down, taking him, battering him. He let go, released the tension of fighting, and willed the other tension to take its place. The first pulses of her release arrived, squeezing his cock. She drove harder, thrashing against him with a fiendish energy. Within seconds, the chill of her flashed through him, flash freezing the depths of his body. Icing his soul. For those seconds he ceased to exist. He hung in the balance between good and evil. Between whom he once was and who he would someday become.

He accepted the impossibility of his own nonexistence and was rewarded by an explosive wave of deep decadence. He grunted, moaned, and panted, willed the circle of cruel carnality to take even more of him. Now grinding his teeth, wanting, needing the pleasure-pain to be finished. He couldn't breathe; he couldn't think. He could only toss his head, grind his teeth and wait.

And he was delivered.

The final release ripped through him, its wrath so fierce that for that long second it promised to tear out his heart, with all its fresh pain and confusion, straight from his chest. He stayed there in that silent emotionless abyss for several seconds before falling, crashing, back. Above him, she was now grinding through her own release, her face contorted, her own jaw tight, clenching as she threw her head back and succumbed to her own moment of vulnerability. Her flash of weakness was always quicker than his, and soon she returned to herself and the reality of their lives.

She grunted, stood, and pulled her pants up.

Hayden's hands were still shaking, his stomach still trembling, as he grabbed at his own clothing, struggling to pull his briefs up and then his pants. By the time he got to his feet, she was already sitting on the edge of the desk, legs crossed, booted feet swinging. He stood before her with his pants unzipped, his clothes not yet back in place.

Uncharacteristically silent, she was staring out the window, her gaze taking in the final, hazy lines of the smothered sun as it dipped behind the buildings surrounding them. The sky, now completely full of gray clouds, promised another night of rain. Hayden picked up the chair, righted it and then rolled it under the desk. Once it was back in place, he finished straightening his clothes. Now well accustomed to Mattie's quick shift from fucking to not fucking, he took his time repairing the damage to his appearance, body, and mind. She, on the other hand, seemed to have already forgotten their violent coupling.

"And so?" he asked, moving to the window, peering out. Off in the distance, a bus rounded a corner, nearly hitting a white minivan that had run the light. He wasn't the only one living dangerously.

"You really haven't figured out what brought me here. I mean," she gestured to his crotch, "aside from your obvious charms and talents."

He refused to acknowledge that he did have a choice now, whether to fuck her. But he set that aside and dove in. "The move from the camp?" He pointed to the articles. "Elizabeth knows about it. We're working on the request that came through Bob." Not that he wanted to do Bob's bidding. That tie should have been cut. But apparently, Elizabeth sometimes did him favors in return. Or to be more accurate, told Hayden to do the favors for Bob.

"Not that." She grabbed her jacket from the floor. "Aren't you concerned for your gaudy girlfriend? Don't you miss her?"

Whether or not Rachelle was actually his girlfriend was up for debate, but he knew better than to waste his energy. Miss her? No. Felt guilty about what had happened to her? Yes. Even though he shouldn't. She'd asked for what'd happened to her. Demanded it, actually. Then, like everything else in her privileged life, she got it. "I'm pretty sure she stopped being my girlfriend the day I met you."

"Not my fault." She laughed. "It gets worse. Rumor is her daddy is looking for her."

Hayden snorted. Fucking rich people. She'd been gone for months. "Did he just now notice she hasn't been around?"

"Oh? You think that's funny? Seems to me you'll be a person of interest if she is reported missing."

"Grab some oil and turn her. Nobody will notice anything. They sure as hell won't notice the change in her personality." It was his turn to laugh.

She hopped off the desk, picked up her jacket, then came to stand beside him at the window. "Matthew didn't bring her with the others."

"Why not?" He kept his gaze on the street, watching the blur of lights from the rush hour traffic. "I thought she was his special favorite."

"Turns out he's mad at her for what she did to me. At least that's what he said... to me."

Hayden wasn't about to attempt to understand Mattie and Matthew's destructive and disgusting relationship. "He participated. They both did that to you."

She lifted her chin and stared down at him, her mouth curled into a sneer. The look was a reminder that he too was part of the ritual that made her into a dormant.

She shoved her arms into her jacket. "He blames her."

"Are you saying he left her behind?"

"I went to the bunker yesterday; all the shelves are

15

empty. All of them are gone." She zipped up her jacket. "Everything is gone. Everyone is moved out. The whole camp is empty."

"Seems you need to do a better job keeping track of your... bodies."

She grabbed his stack of articles, started flipping through. When she came to the list he'd started, she picked it up, reading the listings aloud.

He interrupted her. "You going to go to every abandoned building in the city? Crawl around in the basements? Climb into the attics? Think you'll find her that way?"

"It's your life that is about to get fucked. Well, more fucked. So, you're the one who ought to be looking for her." She dropped the list onto the desk, then left.

Chapter Two

"It's your life that is about to get fucked."

Late Friday afternoon, Nidhi Bansal jogged up the Boston Public Library's interior golden marble stairs, her messenger bag thumping against her spine as the pair of stately stone lions, poised above, glared down from the corners of their eyes. Judging. Mocking. Remembering her from before those trips to rehab, back when she was a kind, respectable girl, one of the library's most dependable and friendly tour guides. She reached the top landing, whirled around the corner, the lions' gazes taking her in one last time before she started down the hallway. This library, formerly one of her favorite places, was one of the spots she'd been avoiding since reemerging from her chemically induced isolation. Now though, she couldn't avoid it any longer. Somewhere on the shelves sat a book that could validate her emerging theory that cults recruited from fandoms. She'd shared her developing theory with her grad advisor, and the professor supported the possibility of including the concept into her dissertation proposal. Nidhi needed evidence. The newly emerging fandom, the Tribexxers, were going to give it to her.

She ducked into Bates Hall, pausing to take it all in, knowing she was right back where it started. Not for her, but for him. Hayden, Hume's wonder boy. The newly minted cool kid who'd kicked up all the dusty excitement, gotten mixed up with the seedy underbelly of the living, breathing beast that was one of Boston's oldest, and wealthiest, social circles. Then he did the unforgivable. He exposed the deviant crowd through his articles for Bob Keeler's ludicrous tabloid rag, *The Boston Weekly*. Then got hired at *The Globe*. The way it looked to Nidhi, that move up was their way of shutting him up.

Sure, the talk around town about the local rich being linked to a zombie-themed sex club was built on speculation and rumors, but still, the elite did not like to be talked about in such an unattractive way. The wealthy set was even more unhappy about the new fast-growing local fandom, the Tribexxers. For some reason, the socialites took the existence of the goth-inspired, zombie pretenders as an offense to their elevated social standing. All that unhappiness was good news for her though, it played right into her own research on fandoms. The whole exploding scene provided her the perfect opportunity for microsociological research right there in her hometown. Bonus for her, she had a vendetta. That world had torn her apart, and she was looking for an opportunity to return the favor.

The library's legendary Bates Hall was as Hayden had described it in that first outrageous article—row after row of gleaming wood tables each topped with green shaded lamps. The sand-colored domed ceilings at the end, the matching ornate arches that ran the length of the room, so beautiful. So elegant. The now-infamous high backed captain's chairs punctuated the tables, making the place look oh-so-intellectual.

Nidhi saw more than those simple things; she saw

evidence of the history she'd studied and talked about back when she'd worked at the library. She knew more than Hayden did, too, about those predatory, ultra-rich social circles. She'd grown up right smack in the middle of one, and she had the battle scars, literal and figurative, to show for it. Hence, the desire for retribution. Right then, though, Nidhi wanted to see the room as he had seen it. Set aside her own experiences and spot something everyone else had overlooked.

"Your fancy university library isn't good enough for you? You have to come slumming here?" The familiar, eager whisper came from right beside her. "Do you need some help?" It was the security guard, the one they'd all called Creepy Ken. Creepy for obvious reasons. Ken because nobody bothered to remember his name.

"I don't need any help." Not from him, anyway.

"No? You already have," he tapped his badge, "all the badass security you can handle?"

She looked past him. Should she start there, in Bates Hall, search for some sort of clue, or head to the nonfiction section and look for the book? Which would be a better way to shake Ken off? More importantly, if someone were actually looking for her, where would they start? Then again, maybe she could get some use out of the guard. "Have you seen anyone... unusual... today?"

Creepy Ken's gaze slid off her to glide around the room, taking in the smattering of typical library patrons—old guys jotting in notebooks, teens tapping on screens, and college students somehow managing to look frantic while sitting in place. That last set of patrons she could relate to. She'd been there. Done that. Earned herself a graduate degree, got into the PhD program, got herself clean, started her research. Next up, a career of her own

19

creation. Step by step, she'd find her way out of that top-tier, tight-knit social circle so many people thought they wanted to get inside.

The security guard's dense features pulled together in full concentration as he scanned the room, seeking with an unwarranted intensity, as though spotting someone unusual would earn him a prize. Thanks to the constant downpours that'd been drenching the city, the room had fewer patrons than usual. His eyes came back to her quickly, and he shrugged, the slight motion delivering a whiff of Axe body spray. Apollo scent. The same one her high school boyfriend wore. Attempting to channel some of her own now long-gone high school innocence, she pulled her mouth into a smile and whispered again. "Not in here." She gestured behind her, moving her index and middle finger like a pair of legs. "I mean creep—walking around."

He pinched the sleeve of her gray trench coat between his fingers, then pulled as she moved away, urging her to follow him to the corner by the elevator. Never in the past would she ever let herself be caught in a secluded area with this guy, but needy times called for desperate measures. She went along with him, her fake smile fading despite her effort to continue using it. He backed her into the corner then planted his palm on the wall. His bulky body blocked her view. His canned smell smothered her.

"So, you want something unusual? I can be unusual."

"I don't want *something*. I'm looking for—"

Her words evaporated. Brown leather pants, smeared with rainwater, battered black boots leaving a trail of mud on the smooth, century old floor. Her mouth twitched. Creepy Ken's gaze dropped to her lips, and his mouth curled upward.

"Yeah? Nidhi? What're you looking for?"

The body, just feet away, moved closer still then paused near the archway into Bates Hall. Her breath hung in her lungs. The heavy, leather boots, the staple of every Tribexxer, close enough now that she could hear the wet squeak of the soles on marble. The security guard must have mistaken the panic in her eyes for some sort of sexual interest. He lifted his eyebrows and ogled her.

Above them, the lights blinked off, stayed off.

After several seconds, he muttered, "Fuck," then dropped his arm and lifted his chin. "Fucking storms. Fucking generators." He studied the ceiling, then twisted to glance behind himself. Mumbling again, he grabbed the flashlight from his belt, flicked it on and stepped into the hall, toward the entryway to Bates Hall.

Once he was out of sight, she leaned forward. There was no shadow nearby. No boots squeaking in the dim light. Nidhi slid out of the corner, inching her way toward the landing she'd come up. Just as she reached the top of the stairs, the guard reappeared. He looked beyond her, leaning over to search the stairs and lower landing. Nidhi's fingers were on the rail, her heart hammering. The lights blinked on, stayed on for a few seconds, then went off again.

Creepy Ken, oblivious to her distress, cast her an annoyed glance as though the power surges were her fault. "Gotta do some rounds," he said, his voice resonant with self-importance. "You know, make sure things are alright." He strutted forward but just as quickly stopped short and looked back toward her. "Come back and see me again." He patted the keys dangling from his belt. "All access baby. We'll find us a quiet place and work out that kink you have." He grunted then stalked off, disappearing down the stairs.

Her stomach rolled. The guy was disgusting. How had he managed to keep his job all these years?

She lingered on the landing. A bolt of thunder so loud she could hear it through the thick, old exterior walls was followed by a crack of lightning that bolted above the library's courtyard. It streaked through the sky, visible through the large panes of glass above the Grand Staircase. Rain pattered against the arched windows, smearing the glass with disturbing splotches of water, alive with the storm. If the power remained a problem, would they evacuate the building? She'd hide in the bathroom, wait until the building was empty, then she'd have hours to search for the book. Could she get that lucky?

The lights in Bates Hall had been off long enough that the soft conversational rumble of the library patrons drifted outward. She knew from experience, only the most dedicated, or desperate, would be at the library on a rain-stormy Friday afternoon. Her best guess, most of them would wait it out, stay put until the generators kicked on. She wasn't going to stay put. If she did, she ran the risk of coming up against Creepy Ken or worse, the man in the leather pants. Even if all he sought was a confrontation of some sort, she didn't have the time or interest. She took another glance behind her, then went toward the nonfiction section, double checking the screen shots of the catalog numbers as she headed toward the shelves. The underground book she sought had to be in the same stack or in the same general area as Guy Belmont's now legendary zombie tribe ethnography.

That book wouldn't be there; it was long gone for sure. Probably sold on eBay for enough to pay off someone's overdue rent. But the other one, the one he'd published under a pseudonym, that one could be right there on one of the shelves.

Her phone buzzed.

A message was from Hume.

Need you back here.

She took a few more steps, then paused. Her fingers hovered over the letters, wanting so badly to write *fuck you and your dumb job too*. But it wasn't time for that. Not yet.

Before she could write anything, another message popped up.

I know it's raining. But come now.

Raining? Another rumble followed by a loud, vibrating clap. Only Hume would call that rain.

Nidhi dropped her phone back into her jacket pocket. She secured her bag, pulled up her hood, backtracked to the Grand Staircase landing, then descended the steps, again passing under the watchful gaze of the lions. Once through the door that opened out onto Dartmouth, she reached the bottom of the entrance steps before stopping short.

Unbelievable, but there they were. Together. The two of them, a mismatched pair of creepiness, walking, nearly running, away from the library building. The leather pants, the black boots, the allover angsty vibe, her hunch had to be correct, the guy was one of them. The Tribexxer was in front, his face up, rain pounding against him as he moved. Creepy Ken hurrying behind, his short arms swinging wildly as he strutted along, trying to catch up to the long-legged man. Finally, one of the guard's hands got close enough to tap the corner of the other man's leather jacket. The other man dipped away, slipping inside the bus shelter. Ken was still talking, his face contorted as he spewed whatever stupid shit he had on his mind.

Nidhi backed up the few steps she'd come down, then flattened herself against the side of the building. The eave far above offered only slight protection from the downpour, but enough so that she could see better. The two of them, together, in the bus shelter locked in argument, words tumbling from each of their mouths, simultaneously, as though they were singing a bad duet. Suddenly, they both stopped talking. Stopped moving. The guard's head tipped sideways toward the library. The Tribexxer's head swiveled, his gaze cutting through the sheets of rain, searching.

A tight wire of fear wove itself around Nidhi's whole body, pulled tighter and made her shiver. Common sense reminded her that no one knew she was looking for the book. No one knew about her online research, including her @ersatzTgurl twitter handle. She'd gone to great lengths to make sure nothing she posted made her personally identifiable. She hadn't told anyone about her quest for the sought-after secret book or the account, not even Easton, her best friend.

As much as she wanted to, needed to, she had yet to meet any of the members of the zombie fandom in person. Sure, people made jokes about the sex cult zombies and their fucked-up ways. But she knew there was some truth in the rumors, and that was what she aimed to uncover— what was true, what wasn't. People clung to the idea of a tribe of zombies being a cult because it was both hilarious and frightening. Obviously, the crap about the zombies was simply something Hayden cooked up to make money for Bob Keeler. But the part about the city's wealthy being involved in some sort of NXIVM sex cult—there was something to that.

She was focusing on where the new fandom ended and the other group began. How the pieces fit together. How social status and social roles fit into the overall structure. And, most importantly, who among Boston's rich elite was involved and how. That's why she needed to get her hands on Belmont's secret research. Her career plan was also why she needed to stay out of trouble while getting that book. Top universities did not hire from a pool of sex-scandal-soaked candidates. They hired from a pool of respectable scholars.

Nidhi tensed, waited until both their heads were turned toward Dartmouth, then shoved off the wall and ran. Cold, fat, sideways raindrops came in under her hood. The rivulets made their way down the sides of her neck, slithering deep down underneath her coat. A river of shivers ignited her skin. She fought against the small tremors as she dashed through the sheets of rain, jumped the curb. The water in the road was rushing too fast for puddles to form. There was a river flowing down the street. Her feet splashed water upward, drenching her tights as she scurried from the building toward the T stop.

Like everyone else in the subway car, she was soggy and subdued. The car rumbled along, sometimes shaking, sometimes smooth, flashing lights followed by darkness. Her gaze dropped to the rivulets on the floor, changing directions with the car's motion. Some would say she was lucky to have such an extraordinary life, one that included placement in a prestigious PhD program, a part time gig at *The Boston Globe*, a posh townhouse on Acorn Street in Beacon Hill, a conditional courtesy from her parents, and now—an adventurous demanding sex partner. That last bit was something others weren't yet envious of because she hadn't told anyone about that new development in her life. Maybe, if things went the way she hoped, they'd be more than just partners with sex. But for now, business before pleasure, and so the impromptu meeting with Hume.

The early spring rain was still coming hard and fast when she came up the stairs at the other end. Nidhi accepted the drenching as she completed her dash from one historical Beantown building to another. The outside of *The Globe*'s headquarters wasn't all that impressive, and so as she rushed up the steps, she didn't bother to admire the exterior. Once inside, she paused in the downstairs hallway to take off her bag and shake off her coat. People came out of the elevator, pulling on raincoats and popping up umbrellas as they rushed past. She scooted to stand beside the wall so she could roll her wet coat into a ball. She stuffed it into her bag.

Upstairs, the front room of her boss's office was empty. Darrel, Hume's well-polished, red-haired guard dog, or dare she say it—ultra-efficient boy toy—who usually sat at the desk, gone too. Usually, she took the opportunity to chat with him, lively office gossip that he was, and squeeze out whatever unofficial information she could. This time though she was glad to see the desk vacant. All she wanted right then was to answer Hume's call, get the details on the new assignment, then leave. She swung the bag's strap up over her shoulder, plastered on a professional smile, then stepped into her boss's office.

The prepared smile vanished as quickly as she'd assembled it. She froze, hand lingering on the doorknob until she finally decided closing the door was the better option. That way, if the boss did show up, there would be a few seconds to right the wrong she'd walked into.

"Crafty bitch, aren't I?"

Mattie.

The other girl was seated on top of Hume's mid-century desk, her powerful, bare legs swinging, her boots dangling above the pure beige carpet. A single dirty drop of rainwater fell from one of the heels, landing silently, leaving a tiny stain.

"Oh, hey." An unexpected and unexplainable trickle of fear drizzled down Nidhi's spine. The urge to open the door again, peek into the exterior waiting room, made her fingers twitch.

Mattie scooted backward, rolling her solid hips across the polished cherry wood, then slowly crossed her legs, giving Nidhi a peek at her bare crotch. "That's all you have to say, baby?" She shaped her lips into an exaggerated pout. "I assumed you liked my extra-naughty side."

"I—I thought… Hume texted me." Nidhi let out a crafted puff of frustration, one she hoped hid her mix of fear and annoyance. "Beckoned me to do her bidding. Know what I mean?"

The pout was gone and in its place was a leer. "Yes," her voice was softer now. Gentle but hungry. "I know exactly what you mean."

That eerie dangerous, uncontrollable heat, the one she was beginning to associate with Mattie, came crawling back. *All the way in*, that's how Mattie had encouraged her that first night they'd gotten together. At the time, that'd sounded sexy and exciting. Now…

Nidhi set down her bag, forced her hands to stay loose

by her sides, then in a lame attempt to look casual, leaned against the door. When the other girl's intense gaze became too much, she turned her own to the window. The storm had softened to a drizzle, but the clouds were so thick the sky was a haze. "The lady is bound to pop back in here. She must've had a reason for texting me."

"I texted you." Mattie held Hume's phone in her long, pale fingers. "Don't look so surprised, baby." She shimmied, making her huge breasts jiggle beneath the tight white T-shirt, then mimicked a body check. "It was a simple matter of bumping into her in the hall and snatching her phone out of her bag. That woman should get her shit together. She runs part of this very serious newspaper. People depend on her." She opened her palm, and the phone fell. The device landed near the edge of the desk, teetered, then dropped to the floor with a soft thud. "Whoops, looks like your boss dropped her phone on the floor. Left it at work."

Nidhi had considered flirting with Mattie the day in the bathroom, when she'd figured out the girl was hooked up with Hayden. In the end, though, she hadn't had to make the decision whether or not to act on impulse because the other girl came onto her first. A week ago, Mattie had propositioned her in the elevator and then followed her outside. Out on the sidewalk, she'd convinced her to go with her to a nearby bar. In the end, she'd gotten more than a good time. She'd gotten some very valuable information. She'd been getting more of both ever since. Maybe though, those good times came with a price.

"I must say, you look awkwardly sweet all wet like you are."

Nidhi waved one hand toward the door. "Want to get out of here? Go someplace?"

"I like it here. Don't you?"

Now the rain had completely stopped, the sky was still with a greenish hue. Bleak clouds hung high in the sky, a thick band of foreboding.

Mattie made a deliberate display of uncrossing her legs, then recrossing them, the flex of her muscles and the roll of her hips an intimidating seduction. "This desk is pretty solid. I like that. A solid desk that can take a beating is pretty important." She swung her leg, kicking one of the legs with the heel of her boot. "We'd expect this sort of high-quality furnishing from Hume, right?"

"I guess so," she replied, even though she had no idea what Mattie was getting at.

"Don't you know? Hume's husband is an interior designer. Kind of famous for it, actually."

"No, I didn't know that." Nidhi studied the desk. It did have that expensive look she knew so well. "I didn't even know she was married."

"Well, baby?" She planted her hands behind herself, arching her back, shoving her tits upward. "I told you; your boss was on her way home. Probably feeding her cat by now. No worries." There was no denying the message. The girl wanted what she wanted, and she wanted it right then. Right there.

Even if Hume was gone, there was the janitorial staff.

Maybe she was overthinking this. The possible presence of other people was part of the excitement. Right? It could be, anyway, if she let herself feel it.

"I thought you were adventurous." Mattie shoved herself forward, sat up straight and looked at the door. "Am I going to be disappointed?"

Chapter Three
"Crafty bitch, aren't I?"

Nidhi stepped forward, meeting Mattie at the edge of the desk. "I don't want you to be disappointed."

"After what you said about Hume fucking with you all the time, I thought this," she nodded to the desk, "would be a fitting start at revenge."

Revenge? Is that what she wanted? Not if it involved her getting fired. Still, she didn't want to lose this new... *relationship* wasn't the right word. Release? Means to an end? Neither was very kind but both fit.

Mattie hopped off the desk, grabbed Nidhi by the waist and spun them both around. "You first, schoolgirl." She lifted her onto the desk. The easy action a reminder of Mattie's compelling, unnatural strength.

"Schoolgirl?" She laughed, even to her the mirth sounded forced.

"That dress, tights, and those rainboots." Mattie grabbed the hem of her dress and tugged it upward. "Where were you?" she asked.

Nidhi reached down, and their fingers touched. An electric flicker of anticipation ran up Nidhi's arm. It was definitely excitement, she told herself, not angst. Mattie had the hem up around her waist and was reaching for the band of her plum-colored tights. No panties under the tights, so once the thin layer of knit was down... "I was at the library," she said, trying to slow things down. "I was looking for Guy Belmont's other book."

"Aren't you the curious kitten." Mattie tucked her fingers into the waistband. "Find it?"

Their eyes were level, their mouths close. "Nope."

"Too bad."

"It sure would help if I knew the title or the fake name."

"Yeah. It sure would."

The green from the sky reflected in the other girl's eyes, giving them an eerie emerald gleam. Nidhi leaned forward, pressed her mouth to Mattie's. Soft on firm. She urged Mattie's mouth open, explored the recesses with her tongue and waited for the flicker of longing she should feel. Wanted to feel. Mattie copied the motion, her tongue exploring Nidhi's mouth, sweeping across her teeth and taking control of the kiss. This is the spontaneity her life had always been lacking. So, she succumbed, compelling herself to relax, willing herself to enjoy it.

Mattie ended the kiss; Nidhi opened her eyes.

The sky was darker, the sun blocked by the clouds. Somehow, the green hue still shone in the other girl's eyes. Gleamed. Mattie broke eye contact by grabbing Nidhi's hips and yanking her forward. The power of the other girl sent a bolt of shock through her, and that fear returned, weaving itself around Nidhi. Hume walking in, firing her. Not likely. Security cameras, catching all this. No, not in the office. Then there was Mattie, the unknown and maybe unknowable, woman tugging her tights down over her bare thighs, her mouth just inches from her crotch. Only a few licks away from her pussy.

Yes.

31

She must want it. There was no reason not to. Yet…

"That's a good girl." The compliment was a melancholy purr.

For a fleeting second, Nidhi considered whether the praise was deserved. She hadn't done anything other than let the other girl do what she wanted. She'd done that sort of thing, giving in to the wants of others, before. Plenty of times. It was how she'd gotten through high school. And most of undergrad. During rehab she'd made the promise to herself that she'd never fake it again. Was this faking it?

Nidhi murmured.

Mattie separated her legs.

Nidhi stiffened.

Mattie's mouth connected with her skin. She started with an undemanding row of kisses on her thighs, then moved inside, gently using her lips to nip Nidhi's pussy lips, then worked her way in, finding her clit and giving it a quick soft flick that should have felt good. Nidhi stared at the sterile white ceiling. Mattie continued eating her pussy, alternately sucking and flicking her clit.

"You are a stubborn thing today, aren't you?" Mattie slid her palms underneath Nidhi's ass, taking one cheek in each hand. She squeezed, kneaded the flesh, then lifted her hips off the desk even as she continued to flick her clit with her tongue. This had to be what she'd been seeking. Thrilling, risky, exploration. The chance to be *improper*. Be the sort of person who broke rules and didn't care what other people thought. Nidhi felt the first thread of pleasure and she clung to it, willed the tiny flame to grow big, take her over.

Mattie lowered Nidhi's ass and lifted her mouth. "Now you want it, don't you? I'm glad. I was beginning to think you didn't like me." She dove back, attacked both Nidhi's ass and her pussy. The assault grew rougher, more intense, almost animalistic, and it took all of Nidhi's concentration to hold onto the pleasure and push back the fear. One way or another she had to come.

Once she came, it would be over.

Nidhi clenched her teeth, squeezed her jaw, and closed her eyes. Gradually the tension grew, the familiar stiffness clutched her, tightening gradually until the first flickers of her orgasm arrived, taunting, pausing, pulling, prodding, then crawling inside her, heating her pussy, breaking her will to reason and then taking a slice of her soul as it fluttered, then went.

Once the last pulse of cruel pleasure passed, Mattie lifted her mouth, righted herself, wiping her lips with the back of her hand as she looked down. The green sheen in her eyes was gone. Her face seemed brighter. More relaxed. Why the hell had Nidhi been afraid? Stress was getting to her. She needed to take some time off. She needed to get back to yoga or meditation. She needed… something.

Needed.

She lifted herself from the desk and reached for Mattie's shoulders. "Your turn."

Mattie grinned as she dodged Nidhi's touch. "It is my turn, but I want something different." She moved toward the door, reached for the doorknob, then turned back, watching Nidhi as she slid from the desk and righted her clothes. The tense sense of excitement was already gone, the carnality of the orgasm a memory.

"Different?" That could mean a lot of things and Nidhi was starting to think she may not want to do some of them.

"So, you owe me. Okay, baby?" She slipped out the door without waiting for a reply.

* * *

Instead of getting off at the stop closer to her townhouse, Nidhi took the T to Boylston. Up on the street, she headed in the opposite direction of the traffic, pausing as she often did when she walked through her neighborhood after work, at the Central Burying Ground. She set her fingers on the black wrought iron railing and examined the cemetery, gloomy and forlorn even on bright spring days. A patch of land time had forgotten. The whole place was still, gloomy, and damp from the rain. The thunderstorm had knocked branches loose, so occasional limbs and larger branches were scattered across the ground. The narrow dirt path that cut through the centuries-old resting place was dotted with tiny puddles. The usual squirrels had yet to climb from their nests.

The dappled headstones, sagging into the earth at varying angles, had always intrigued her. Not many tourists came by this cemetery, but the ones who did looked for the Chinese teenager Chow Manderien or poet Charles Sprague. Many of the slabs had engravings so time-worn it was impossible to tell who lay beneath the soil. Those people were long forgotten. Yet their descendants lived, somewhere, roaming the planet and very much alive. Some of them, most likely not even knowing that they had an ancestor planted in the historic graveyard. That was the researcher in her, always wondering, questioning. The human side of her felt quite different. If she was being honest, the place did more than intrigue her. It made her skin tingle.

She let go of the fence and took the path north, alongside Charles Street to cut through the park. The baseball field was abandoned. There was no line at the souvenir stand. She reached the end of the park. Small currents of water rushed alongside Beacon Street, and she had to jump from the curb to avoid getting splashed by the cars crossing through the intersection. The storm had eased up. People were back on the street hustling, moving, getting back to what remained of the day. In typical East Coast fashion, they all pretended the death-defying thunderstorm had never happened. It, like that rushed sexual interlude in Hume's office, was a vague memory.

Nidhi pulled out her phone and hit Easton's number. He answered on the second ring, barking hello into the receiver. The roar of printing presses groaned behind him, clanking rhythmically.

"Aren't you out of there yet?" she asked, holding the phone away from her ear as she reached her corner.

He yelled something that sounded like hold on a minute. She held the phone to her ear as she continued walking. The multi-colored cobblestones running down the center of Acorn Street were shimmering from the rain, and she knew from experience to be careful. A sign, slippery when wet, would be useful and correct but would ruin the quaintness of one of the most photographed streets in the US. She stayed on the thin brick sidewalk that ran the length of both sides of the narrow street, but it too was treacherous in its own, uneven, way. She lowered the phone so that she could dig her keys from the outer pocket. When she put it back to her ear, the churning sounds of the machines were continuing to grow distant. Finally, the noise was mostly a background hum.

"Got started late," he said, now talking at a normal decibel.

Nearing her own door, she spotted a brown lump on her welcome mat.

35

She continued forward. "There's a package on my doorstep."

"The way you say that it doesn't sound like it came from Amazon."

She stood before it, examining the battered edges. "I didn't. I haven't ordered anything in weeks."

"Does *The Globe* have a bomb squad?" Excitement pitched his voice upward. "Is someone out to get you?"

He meant it as a joke, but after seeing that Tribexxer and Creepy Ken together, the idea made her stomach turn. The idea of them blowing her up was ridiculous, of course, but—

"You know the cops leave bombs on people's steps to trick them into touching them. Once the package has your fingerprints on it, they arrest you."

"What the fuck are you talking about?"

"I saw a thing about it on YouTube."

The brown paper wrapped package on her doorstep sagged from the rain. The soaked paper looked like wrinkled skin. "You know that YouTube is not a legitimate information source." A scent drifted under her nose, so sharp and sudden she tasted it far back in her mouth. Turning, she sniffed the air. Was the smell floating up from the wet cobblestones? Or from the package?

"Not all of us side-hustle for *the* paper."

She tapped the package with her toe. The edges were firm. Despite the wrinkled paper, the package had some weight. Not much, though.

He continued. "I guess the cops aren't going to fuck with you fancy folks on Acorn Street."

Fancy folks, that was her. Four million dollars could have bought a lot more somewhere else, but thanks to her parents and their love for real estate investments, there she was in Instagram friendly Beacon Hill. Cozy shops and rich couples pushing thousand-dollar strollers. That was her neighborhood. "No, they are certainly not going to fuck with us." Thanks to all the tourists clicking selfies and trying to see what all the fuss was about, the short street wasn't quiet, but as far as its residents went, she had to be the youngest person on the historic block by decades.

"So, you don't think it's a bomb? Retribution for something you wrote?"

Typical Easton, always drawn to drama. But something about the question made her grasp something she should have already understood. "Hume mostly uses me for articles about rich people and their giant stacks of money."

"Kind of makes sense, seeing as you know more about that than anyone else in that office. I get your point though. Nobody is going to blow you up for telling the world about their worthy project or massive donation."

Blowing someone up wasn't the move of a fandom either. So why the creepy-crawly feeling racing up and down her arms? She looked over her shoulder. The drizzled brick sidewalks were empty. The cobblestone road was vacant. The lone American flag, down at the end of the short street, fluttered idly in the slight breeze. The only visible life belonged to some pansies and other plants filling the window boxes hanging between a pair of wide, ultra-traditional black shutters. She looked the other direction. No one. Nothing to link to the smell or the prickly sensation traveling up and down her arms

"How big is it?" he wanted to know.

She bent low, breathed in, and then flipped it over. The smell wasn't coming from the package. "Shoe box size."

"Addressed to you?"

"No, nothing. No address, no writing at all. It's tied with brown string." She pinched the twine between her fingers and lifted it high above her head. Underside, also blank. A single drop of rainwater rolled down her wrist.

"Old school. My grandfather used to do that. Tie stuff with strings."

She sighed. "Really Easton? Who the fuck cares?"

"You going to open it?"

Ugh. The smell. "Yeah, of course, I—"

The soft thud of a footfall. She stiffened, moving only her eyes as she scanned the street again. The faint movement was at the other end of the street, where picturesque Acorn dead-ended into Willow. Back, moving in the shadows, it vanished. It could be yet another tourist, waiting until the coast was clear so they could peek in windows or take a selfie on one of the stoops. The shiver running down her spine told her otherwise. The Tribexxer followed her home. Impossible. Right?

"I have to call you back."

"Nah, I'm out of here soon. Text me later if you want."

She dropped the phone into her bag and unlocked her door. Once inside, she set the rain-tattered box on the small hall table, then set her bag underneath. She leaned against the door, her hands shaking as she slid the rarely used deadbolt into place. She shrugged out of the trench coat, draped it over one of the nearby hooks, then sat on one of the steps leading upstairs to tug off her dripping rain boots. Tea first, then she'd deal with the box.

After she had the second boot off, a soft knock on her bolted door canceled her trip to her kitchen. She scooted to the front window that looked out onto the street and peeked under the blinds she always left down. Her surprise quickly turned to annoyance. She released the deadbolt then yanked open her front door.

"Hayden?"

Chapter Four

"That's a good girl."

"Not much of a greeting," he said, his expression bland as usual. Behind him, the sky was a gloomy gray. The sun was almost down.

"How do you know where I live?"

"The personnel directory. The one do-gooder Darrel keeps on his desk."

She eased up on the hostility. "It's been a long… stressful … day." Not a lie and maybe enough to soften her abrupt greeting.

"Can I come in?" He leaned forward, his brown eyes focused on the opening between the door and the doorframe. "I won't take long. Please?"

The package, now creating a puddle on her small hall table, waited. "Just a minute."

She shut the door, grabbed her coat then laid it across the table, then opened the door again, stepping back. Inside, he immediately bent down to unlace his boots. She started to tell him he wouldn't be staying long, but he already had one off and was working on the other with a speedy efficiency she wouldn't have thought possible from him. He stood before her in his sock feet, his hands shoved in his brown canvas coat pockets. Other women thought he was good-looking, with deep brown eyes, wavy chestnut hair, and a sturdy square build, but she'd been down that road. It wasn't for her.

"Would you like to sit down," she asked, gesturing to the brocade sofa and hating herself for immediately falling into such a feminine, hostess mode.

He padded over to the sofa, shrugged out of his jacket then sat down, placing his coat over his knees.

She knew she was going to hate herself yet again, but she let the words out. "Would you like some tea?"

He leaned back and tried to peer under the window covering.

"Expecting someone else?" she asked, moving to the hall.

He moved back then patted his coat with his hands. "No, not really."

"I'm going to put the kettle on. For myself." She put emphasis on that second piece of information. "You let me know if you change your mind about the tea." After starting the water, she came back into the room to sit in one of the two chairs across from the sofa. "You didn't come by for tea, so…"

"Yeah." He stopped patting his coat. "I want to tell you something."

"Okay…"

His gaze darted around the room, seeming to take in the charming fireplace, the crammed-to-the-edges built in bookshelves, and the pieces of art her parents had hung. She had no idea what they were, if they were expensive or cheap, and she didn't care. Art had never been her thing. The truth—that was her thing. Well, that and the clear acknowledgement that she was the one who found and delivered that truth.

Staring now at the empty log holder placed beside the fireplace, he said, "I'm trying to help you."

"By coming to my house?"

His attention moved to the unused hand-crafted fireplace tool set on the opposite side. "By what I'm telling you."

Nidhi waited. His gaze shifted back to the fireplace, where three attractively positioned logs sat. Finally, she said, "You haven't told me anything."

He was gazing at the logs now. Unblinking. "I'm about to."

Nidhi hadn't told him anything about her work on the Tribexx fandom, her quest for Belmont's book, or fledgling theory about cults recruiting from fandoms, so whatever he came about couldn't have anything to do with any of that. She pressed her lips shut and willed herself to stay silent.

After another long pause, his head moved. His eyes were unfocused. "It's about... that girl. The one you were talking to on the steps in front of the office. You know... the other night, last week..."

Not surprising that he'd zeroed in on *her*, but it was disappointing. All this show, she would have thought it was about more than jealousy. "You spying on me now, Hayden?"

"I wasn't looking for you. I just happened to leave right after you and just happened to see the two of you on the steps."

"Just happened to?" Sure, she'd done the same just-happened-to-see thing to him a couple times, but she wasn't about to admit it.

He sighed, the life in his eyes returning and some of that rumored verve coming alive in his face. "Yes. And, obviously, I don't need to tell you her name, Mattie."

She nodded. She didn't need to say anything about

the two of them being a couple, past tense. No point in rubbing that little piece of info in his face.

"I could tell by the way the two of you were… talking… that you were getting… acquainted."

That was one way to put it. "Why—"

The shrill whistle of the tea kettle cut through the air. She rose. "Change your mind about the tea?"

He shook his head.

Nidhi used the time in the kitchen to mull things over but came up with nothing other than the obvious. The guy was a sore loser.

Carrying her steaming mug of Chamomile, she came back into the room. "So, you were describing my new acquaintanceship?"

He looked to the floor, stared at his sock feet for several seconds, then slid them under the coffee table. "She isn't… who you think she is."

Letting the tension linger, she lifted her tea, took a sip. She lowered the mug and set it in her other palm. "Oh?"

He squeezed his eyes shut and nodded. "That's right."

"She isn't your *girlfriend*? Because that's who I think—thought—she was."

He opened his eyes as he leaned back, his gaze not as vacant as before. "She isn't my girlfriend." Nidhi watched his face, the twitch of his mouth, the guarded glaze over his eyes. It was a look she'd never seen before, not on anyone.

"You shouldn't have her for your girlfriend either." His voice was soft, his words hardly above a whisper. "She shouldn't be anyone's girlfriend."

The memory of that scene in the office sliced through her mind. The way she'd felt, forcing herself to relax so she would cum, and waiting, wanting for the sex to be over. The expression on his face was beginning to make some sense, but damn if she was going to give up on someone, something, that could challenge her to grow personally and at the same time help her get a successful career. "She's not up to your standards, Hayden? She's a little too... experimental... too... much for you to handle?"

"That is not what I mean. Remember, I'm here to help you. That's why I came.

He moved himself forward, resignation shaping his face. "This is what I wanted to tell you."

"You haven't told me anything."

He reached into his coat pocket, pulled out his phone, checked the screen. "Don't go with her. Don't be with her." He looked up. "That's what I'm telling you."

"Why?"

He slid his phone back into the pocket and scooted forward to stand. "I guess I'm trying to be a nice colleague."

"I don't give a shit about you being a nice colleague. I want to know why she isn't the right girl for me."

He stood. "I can't tell you that."

"You mean you won't tell me." She got up too, still holding the tea.

"It's for your own good."

She took a sip of the tea, smirking over the rim as she swallowed. "Well, aren't you the king of the patriarchs."

"We aren't in competition, Nidhi." He slipped on his coat. His fingers made quick work of the buttons. "We're co-workers."

"Co-workers at a newspaper." Realizing that she'd be seeing him again on Monday, she gentled her voice.

"That automatically puts us in competition. It's the nature of the job."

He made his way to the hall and stepped into his boots. "If you want it to be that way, it will be that way. But remember I told you this, she isn't who you think she is; the situation isn't what you think it is or, I guess, what you hope it is."

She had no response for that. "Thanks for stopping by." Again with the ingrained politeness. She set her mug on the coffee table, then followed him to the entryway.

He stilled, his eyes motionless, searching the air. Or was he smelling it? Fuck, she was really losing it. He reached for the door handle. "Be careful, Nidhi. Whatever you want to happen, whatever you're trying to do, it isn't going to be worth it."

"You'd be the one to tell me that?"

He looked back, his unreadable eyes connecting with hers. "Yes, I am." He slipped out the door. No goodbye. No thanks for the hospitality. So much for his manners.

She leaned out, watched him step carefully across the cobblestones, then she turned in the other direction. A couple was walking one in front of the other, on the opposite sidewalk, each carrying two grocery bags. She looked back to Hayden, but he was gone.

Inside, she engaged the deadbolt.

Nidhi took the package to the kitchen, set it on the island, leaned over it, inspecting it for anything she may have missed. Nothing. There were no markings of any kind. Peeling back the damp paper revealed a brown cardboard box taped shut on all four corners and along both sides. The paring knife she never used for food was within easy reach. She grabbed it, perched on the stool beside the island, then carefully cut through the clear packing tape. Once she had sliced all the way around on the top, she used the point of the knife to pop the top off. Inside was another box, this one made of dark brown carved wood. Carefully, she lifted it out and set it beside what remained of the cardboard. There was no tape on the wooden box, but she did need the knife to loosen the tarnished brass latch.

No wires inside.

Not a bomb.

A collection of long vials, some with what looked to be dried leaves, one with liquid, a tiny notebook, and a single key. There were seven jars, each long and narrow, shaped like test tubes, but with silver screw-on tops. Open one? Smell it? What if it was poisonous? What if the plants weren't leaves but psychedelic mushrooms? Who the hell knows what the liquid could be? Nope, not opening any of those.

The leather covered notebook had a thin red leather band around it. She removed the bind, flipped through. Drawing of plants. Sketches that could be maps. Lists of objects. Lists of what appeared to be the scientific names of plants. Or chemicals? Animals? The second half were lists of what might be names written in code or in another language, each name followed by a row of numbers.

Fuck.

It looked like a subscription box from Hogwarts.

She laid the objects out, side by side. No fucking idea what to do with the lot of it.

She grabbed the wine she'd opened last night, pulled out the stopper and took a swig directly from the bottle. What was the point of using a glass? It would just end up in the dishwasher she never ran. It was long past the time to get out of the wet clothes. She left the collection displayed on the island, took the bottle, sipping as she ascended the stairs, pausing when she got to the second floor. There were two bedrooms on the second floor. The one she used for her home office was on the back side of the building. The other, a guest room for when her parents wanted to stay over, was in the front. She continued up to her bedroom, set the wine bottle on the trunk positioned at the foot of her bed and headed to her walk-in closet.

Another sound, or was it just a sensation, made her pause. Even though she knew she was again letting her nerves get the better of her, she couldn't ignore her intuition that something was wrong. She retreated from her room and jogged down the first flight of stairs.

She took a couple steps into the spare bedroom, spotted the reason for her pause. The window was ajar. The cleaners. Again. As she pulled the sash shut, she made a mental note to tell her mom that the pothead cleaners were raising the heat bill. Again.

She jogged down the second flight, checked the first floor. Everything was exactly as she'd left it. Satisfied, she went up both flights. By the time she reached the top floor, her breath was coming in quick puffs. She paused, this time just outside her room, and listened. The curtain settling into place? A branch scraping a window? She grabbed the wine bottle as she went over to look out onto the balcony that overlooked the alley. Sipping the wine, she scanned the area. The narrow space, quaint and charming—and quiet—just like everything else in her pricey neighborhood.

She picked up the bottle, filled her mouth with the rich Cabernet, and went to her walk-in closet. Moments later, her clothes were off, piled on the floor, and the bottle was almost empty. Wrapped in her black silk baroque robe, she set the wine back on the trunk at the foot of the bed, then picked up her laptop. She settled on her bed, logged on, went straight to #Tribexx, and searched for the latest posts.

The first few were about the event set for Sunday night, the first Tribexx event she was determined to get into. Easton agreed to go with her. Posters were discussing clothes, like which were better, over the knee boots or combat. Suggestions for eye makeup and hair styles. Nidhi skimmed over those and focused on the ones about the organizational plan. Many of the posts appeared to be in code, using hashtags. #yesno and #noyes were the two that still confused her. When she'd seen them in the past, each time the phrase appeared, there was a number beside it and the number continued to escalate until dropping off, then beginning again. Now the hashtags were being used in conjunction with other hashtags such as #spnk and #sub. Those were probably connected to hookups, but she had yet to decipher the specific meanings.

Reluctantly, she realized the long day was starting to get the better of her. Her limbs sagged, and her eyes got heavy. Even her mind was beginning to fade. Her thoughts were blurring together in a way that reminded her of cramming for exams in undergrad, back in the days when she had to deal with the effects of the come down after too much Adderall.

The screen blurred. Nidhi squinted. She adjusted the screen brightness, but still the characters on the screen jumbled together, words sliding into each other, flowing together in an in comprehensible stream. She lifted her hand to close her laptop but missed and knocked it to the floor instead.

Shit.

Giving up on work, she knew she needed to do what her therapist had taught her. So, she laid back onto the pillow, squeezed her eyes shut, rubbed her temples with her fingertips and concentrated on her beathing. In through the nose. Out through the mouth. Again.

And again.

The panic subsided and a cocoon of calm wrapped around her.

"Hey baby. I can see you've been keeping secrets from me."

There was the girl, standing at the foot of the bed, wine bottle in her hand.

"Have you been drinking this right out of the bottle? Kind of low class, especially considering…" She used the bottle to gesture to the antique four poster bed, topped with a custom-made duvet cover, and the walls covered in polished wood paneling accented by intense oil paintings her parents had selected. Even with the lights dim, it was obvious, the place was a fucking showcase of old school Boston beauty. Lush, yes. Expensive, oh hell yes. Nidhi tried to laugh but the sound came out as a gurgle.

"Naughty, naughty, keeping secrets." Mattie's swaying shoulders accentuated the murmur in her voice.

What secrets? The box? Hayden? @ersatzTgurl?

Mattie smirked, then spun in a circle, one arm clutching the wine bottle to her chest, the other out-stretched, fingers pointed to the high-priced everything. "You didn't tell me you're a poor, lonely rich girl. So sad, very sad. All alone in this castle tower."

Nidhi forced out another distorted laugh. "Yeah, whatever."

"Remember how you said it was my turn and remember how I said I wanted something different?"

Mattie shrugged out of her leather jacket, threw it to the floor. "I'm here to tell you what I want." She stepped around to the opposite side of the bed and leaned her hip against the mattress.

She couldn't read Mattie's face. The cozy warmth surrounding her numbed both her body and her mind. Was the other girl trying to be alluring? Mysterious? Playful?

"I want you to take a trip with me." Mattie dropped on to the bed, leaned against the giant gem colored paisley pillows propped against the headboard. The gold tassels bounced as she settled.

Nidhi tried to say she couldn't go anywhere because she had to work, but the words came out in a blur of incoherent syllables.

"Not the sort of trip you're thinking, baby."

It took a few heartbeats for her to process the words, grasp the idea the other girl was putting out. If she'd had access to her feelings, panic would be the frontrunner. Dread right behind.

Mattie rolled forward then crept to the foot of the bed. She sat back on her haunches and grabbed one of the posts. After she wrapped her fingers around the smooth wood, she twisted sideways, reached back, thrust her tits upward. "Give you any ideas?" Again, Nidhi tried to speak but could not. Tried to wake herself up but couldn't.

"I'm glad you have your robe on, already. Makes things nicer for me. I hate the undressing, especially with girls. It makes me feel dirty. Like I'm forcing someone to do something they'd never ever want to do."

She released her hands and crept forward, wriggling

until she was positioned over Nidhi, one leg on each side. The grip of her formidable thighs was enough to pin her down. Placing one hand on each side was enough to keep her from even thinking about trying. "I don't have to worry about that sort of thing with you, though, do I?"

Black fear curled around her, swirling in her stomach, skimming up her arms and down her legs, but her tongue was too heavy. The words weren't there. The only thing in her mouth was the vinegary aftertaste of wine.

"Now you're starting to understand." Mattie pressed a fingertip to Nidhi's lips. "No need to say anything. I know you like me. Want me." She moved her hand away and kissed Nidhi, one long press of the lips. "Nothing's going to change that. Right, baby?"

The truth of the situation gradually slithered to the front of Nidhi's mind. She was already on the trip. Bags packed. Tickets bought. She was already on board the jet plane to Never Ever Land. The one place Nidhi had told herself she would never visit again, but now she was onboard with the door closed. No getting off now.

"We're starting our first trip together, so romantic."

And then Mattie's mouth was over hers, her tongue seeking entry. Nidhi tilted her head back, letting the other woman take the kiss as deep as she wanted, as deep as she needed. The caress of her tongue was aggressive, insistent, and Nidhi allowed that too. The other girl moved above her, the motions causing the sleek silk of her robe to glide across her breasts. Mattie opened the robe, exposing Nidhi's naked body. Once the fabric was fanned around her, Mattie angled herself so that her ass rubbed against Nidhi's pelvic bone and then began rotating her hips. Once around and then again. Around and over again. The circles were slow, tight, but only with a brush of pressure.

"I like that. Keep doing it and grab her tits."

Not Mattie talking. It was a deep voice, from far, far away. Nidhi lifted her head. There was a shadow in the doorway. Tall, black lines that wobbled like a flame, shape shifting as it glided into the room. Mattie kept moving, the rhythmic circles massaging, provoking Nidhi's body. Preparing it. Her center becoming aroused all on its own.

"What took you so long to get here?" Mattie palmed one of her breasts.

Nidhi concentrated all her energy on fighting through the dream. "I…" The words, *I don't want this,* stuck in the back of her throat, buried under the weight of her heavy tongue and dulled spirit.

"He's not going to touch you." Mattie dipped down to pinch Nidhi's other nipple between her lips. The pinching turned into sucking. Mattie lifted her head. "Just pretend he isn't here." She stopped moving and bent down to whisper into Nidhi's ear. "That's what I do. Pretend."

The other person laughed, the sound grew louder, and the shadow closer. "Give me something to watch."

Mattie rose. "I said I would."

Nidhi searched for Mattie but saw only colors, blurred shapes, shifting flashes of skin. Her bedroom had grown cold. Heartless and unfamiliar.

"Where's the phone?"

"There, in my leather on the floor." Mattie replied, "Same unlock code."

And then Mattie was moving again, their bodies merging, then separating. The motions a cold liquid of sex without the desire.

"We're going to make you famous, Nidhi. Won't that be special?"

Nidhi didn't want to be famous. She wanted to be respected. Successful.

"Give me something to feel." That shadow voice again, closer still. Right above.

"I'll give you something better than that. I'll give you something we can use."

The black shadow circled the bed. Nidhi raised one of her arms. Mattie grabbed it and started sucking on her fingertips, the other girl's mouth so cool. Nidhi raised the other, and it was caught by the shadow person's cold hand and pushed upward. She didn't want this, she didn't want any of it, but her body continued to respond to the touches, the caresses, the concentrated care. The vague possibility of fighting drifted through her mind, but she shut it out as quickly as it had come. Her arms were now tied to her bed posts. They'd never let her go, not until they got what they came for.

Nidhi shut off her mind, willing it to go black. It was easy this time, the blackness so nearby that all she had to do was invite it in.

Chapter Five
"I want you to take a trip with me."

A few minutes before midnight, Hayden hustled down the alley, dodging the streams of water rolling from the rooftops and dripping off the branches. Clutching his coat to his chest, he fought both the wind and his misery. The sick feeling in the pit of his stomach was nothing new. The pangs of despair and disgust showed up every time he approached this unmarked back door. It was his body's way of preparing him for what was on the other side, for the world that existed deep inside the building where he'd started his career as a reporter. Look at him now, returning to the same location, only now going in through the back, creeping down into the belly of a beast he'd thought he'd known and then beaten. The ever-evolving situation he'd become part of constantly surprised and shocked him. And pulled him back in. Over and over. Tonight was not an exception.

Bob's personal assistant, Christopher, opened the door. The guy wore his usual bland polo and khakis and flat facial expression. After greeting Hayden, he asked, "Are you joining the others in the lower lounge, Sir?"

Such an elegant way of putting such a hideous thing.

The man ushered Hayden inside, locked the door behind them, then escorted him through the hallway, stuffy from old cigar smoke and the lingering scent of various old-man colognes. The assistant stayed ahead, guiding Hayden even though the two of them had done the same walk many times. They went down a set of stairs, through a pair of metal doors, also locked, until finally stopping at the final door, an intricately carved, wooden one. As he always did, Christopher made a big show of taking the skeleton key from his pocket and unlocking the final door. As far as Hayden could tell, going back and forth through this hallway and managing these doors was a principal task on the guy's job description. Dealing with the worrying whims and disgusting demands of a bunch of gross old men filled the rest of it.

Christopher spread his arms wide. "Make yourself at home."

Hayden stepped into the room. The assistant slipped out; the lock clicked into place when the door shut. With one alarming addition, the space looked the same as it had last time he'd been there. In the center of the room, the usual overstuffed brown leather chairs circled a low round table. In preparation for the planned evening, the bar on the left side of the room was freshly stocked with a bucket of ice, some glasses, and a collection of liquor bottles. Over the months, Hayden had gotten to know who drank from which ones. He drank from none of them. Because he'd seen what the men did with the bottles when they thought no one was looking, he'd adopted the habit of selecting from whatever unopened wine bottle was available. Tonight, there were three bottles of red. He crossed to the bar and grabbed a bottle, a corkscrew, a glass and then carried the lot to the center of the room. He set the glass on the table, dropped himself into one of the chairs and set about the impossible task of adjusting to the new addition to the room.

Behind him, the door opened. Bob came in. He was not attended to by Christopher but instead by low grade movie-star Rod McKinon. Bob wore a wrinkled gray shirt and a pair of equally wrinkled gray pants. His tie was loose, hanging around his neck like an afterthought. Rod wore a black leather kilt. Only the kilt. No shirt. No shoes. No bandana.

Bob, as always, went directly to the bar, grabbed his Johnnie Walker and filled a glass. No time wasting two fingers for him. It was gleaming golden liquid all the way to the top. Rod jogged over to Hayden, the guy's face buzzing from excitement. Or coke. Or from sampling one of the chemical concoctions he crafted in his playroom down the hall. The guy was known for his unusual flexibility and disliked for his constant need to demonstrate it. Hayden didn't have to wait long for the display to begin. The guy twisted himself half around and looked at him over his own shoulder. "Do you like the surprise?"

Hayden made a point of looking at the polished wooden cage in the corner. It was a smaller version of the ones Rod had in his special room down the hall. The thing inside the cage, covered by a sheet of burlap, was asleep or dead. But, of course, these things couldn't die. They can be knocked unconscious, though, and so it could be drugged. Chemical courtesy of Rod, no doubt.

Instead of replying, Hayden turned to Bob who was sticking his fingers deep into the jar of cherries. "Who else is joining us for this little get together?"

The man pulled out a piece of fruit, dropped it into his mouth, and then stuck his fingers back into the jar.

Still digging for another cherry, he spoke around the one in his mouth. "Elizabeth is running late."

"Ohhh." Rod lifted one foot as he raised his arms above his head. He grabbed his foot and pulled it close to his neck. "Lizzie's coming." He dropped his foot and started to grab for the other one.

Bob spit the cherry stem onto the bar top. "Roddy…"

McKinon lowered his leg to the floor and grabbed his long black hair in his fist, smoothing it to one side. "I know, I know."

The old man pointed to the cage and shook his head.

Rod turned to Hayden and spoke in an exaggerated whisper. "I made a promise. So now if I don't behave, Bob will make me take the surprise back to the playroom."

Hayden used the pointed end of the corkscrew to tear the foil on the top of the wine bottle, then focused on getting the cork.

"You should be nicer to me, Hayden. I could tell on you, you know."

Hayden stuck the bottle between his thighs and twisted the screw into the cork. Once he had it out, he looked over at Rod. "Everyone knows I took your shit, and no one cares."

"Matthew would care." Rod had his hands in the low pockets of his kilt. "He'd want to know where you got it. He'd want to know what else I have."

Hayden tipped his head toward the bookshelf that hid the hallway that ran deep under the building. "Do you *want* him to find out what else you have back there?"

"He's not allowed in here." Rod turned a panicked face to Bob. "None of them are."

"No, they are not. Your secrets are safe." Carrying

his glass, now containing three cherries, Bob lowered himself into one of the chairs. The worn leather sagged around him as he settled in and leaned back with a groan.

"I know another reason you should be nice to me, Hayden."

Hayden took a gulp of wine.

"One of your friends would really, really like my special new potion. I thought about giving you some, you know, for you to give her on a special occasion. But I gave it to someone else instead. I thought about using it tonight." He skipped across the room and pointed to a glass vial on the floor next to the cage's door. "But this one is better for Sunday."

"Roddy, stop making a spectacle of yourself. Go get a beer and be quiet." Still with his hands in his kilt's deep pockets, McKinon sauntered across the room. After he dipped behind the bar, the room filled with industrial cyber punk. The gritty rhythm and low hum vibrated around the space. Bob set his drink down and then pulled the wooden box on the table toward him. He flipped it open, withdrew a chubby cigar, then turned the box toward Hayden.

Hayden shook his head. "Not old enough to want to kill myself."

After a snort, Bob pointed and said, "There's only one left. You should take it, so Belmont doesn't get one."

"I don't have the energy to be that vindictive."

Bob glanced up as he was snipping the end of the cigar. "I find that hard to believe."

Hayden poured himself a very full glass of wine, set the bottle down and left it uncorked. It was going to be that sort of night. "I don't care what you believe."

"I find that hard to believe as well." After delivering

his quip, he made a show of lighting the cigar, his fleshy cheeks sinking in with each draw.

"Fuck you, Bob."

Rob, laughing over the Rolling Rock in his hand, sauntered over and sat on the arm of the chair Bob was in.

Hayden sipped his wine. Knowing this crowd, the bottle probably cost more than the accumulated total of his daily expenses, but the quality was wasted on him. The only satisfaction he got from it was the gentle numbing delivered slowly over the course of an evening. That and knowing he didn't have to pay for it. One of these days he'd find out who was footing the bill for this grim social club. Until then, bottoms up.

Bob puffed on his cigar, creating a cloud of high-priced smoke that hung over the table.

Between swallows of beer, Rod swayed side to side as he rolled his sinewy shoulders in rhythm to the electronic music.

As much as he wanted to avoid looking, the lull in action pulled Hayden's attention to the cage and the creature inside it. The thing lay on its side, the top of its head covered by one of Rod's bandanas, a pink one. Its face was turned to the wall, its shoulders curled in. Judging from the size, it was a woman. He wouldn't let himself consider the possibility that it was a child or even a teenager.

The music continued to roll around them, the tobacco fog expanding overhead.

Hayden sipped his wine and stared at the lump of burlap.

The thing moved. At first it was just a twitch. Its spine jerked back. Then a vibration, small thrashing, and quivers. He wanted to look away. He should look away. He didn't.

Rod noticed the movement and set his beer down. "Oh, no. Not yet, baby." He ran to the cage, watched, and waited. It twitched again. He grabbed the vial on the floor, poured some of what was in it onto a rag he'd taken from his pocket and then tossed the freshly doused rag into the cage. The thing's arm slithered out, grabbed the rag and pulled it close. There was some movement and then, nothing. Rod returned, picked up the beer, and perched on the chair.

"All good," he murmured. "Don't want to ruin the surprise." As he downed the rest of the beer, the door swung open. Belmont wandered in. Christopher lingered behind him for a brief second, then turned away, shutting the door with its decisive click. Belmont strolled to the end of the bar and started his own ritual of pouring and mixing.

"Did you have your hands in this jar?" he asked, holding up the half full jar of cherries.

Bob lifted his chin and blew out a stream of smoke.

Belmont shuffled over to inspect Bob's glass, now half empty with one cherry remaining. Two stems were on the floor by Bob's feet. "You did, you disgusting asshole."

"There is a fruit fork on the bar top," Bob said, sliding his foot over the stems.

Belmont flipped open the wooden box and snatched the single remaining cigar. "You've never used a fruit fork in your life." When he returned to the seating area, he carried his usual cocktail minus the usual cherry. "Seems you are still holding a grudge about the article." He took a long drink and looked at Hayden. "He still mad about our article?"

"I wasn't mad." He puffed. "I am not mad." He puffed again. "But I still think it was a stupid move."

"Wasn't stupid at all. I got what I wanted." Belmont lowered his glass. "You think it was stupid Hayden? Seems to me you also got what you wanted."

Yes, the article he and Belmont blackmailed Bob into publishing did get him the notice he wanted. Was he going to admit that? No. He was not getting pulled into their petty old-man bullshit. Besides, was what he got actually what he wanted? Or was it what he needed at the moment? He took a gulp of the wine, dragged his gaze to the cage. None of this was what he wanted.

Belmont picked up the end cutter and went to work on his cigar. "How are things at *The Globe*?"

Hayden, still staring at the contents of the cage, asked, "What do you know about Nidhi Bansal?"

Bob shrugged.

Hayden shifted. "Guy?"

Guy shrugged.

"Pretty girl?" Rod leaned forward. "Smart girl? Dark academia vibe?"

Bob glanced up at Rod. "Dark academia?"

"Yeah," Hayden leaned forward to get eye-to-eye with Rod. "That sounds like her."

"I've seen her at parties. Not much of a dancer, I have to say." Rod tipped his head and frowned. "I talked to her anyway, 'cause I knew she worked with Lizzie, and I was curious, you know, and—"

"What parties?" Hayden asked. "Did you see her at a Tribexx party?"

"Oh no." He snickered. "At rich kid parties. I just saw her at one out in West Roxbury. No dancing at that one. I got her life story. Did you know her parents are rich, rich,

rich? Own a bunch of shit. Rentals, condos, townhomes… anyway… about that party, there was a little fire. Well at first, anyway." He started laughing outright. "She and I kept throwing logs on it and bammo, a bonfire. Such a different crowd from the Tribexxers. They—"

"What the fuck is a Tribexx?" Bob asked.

"I thought that was why you hated the article." Rod smacked Bob's shoulder. "You never listen to me."

Bob's face pulled in.

Hayden lifted his eyebrows at Bob. "But it seems Rod is correct. You don't listen."

"Remember that contest at the convention?" Belmont asked, lowering his unlit cigar. "A couple of the contestants put together a party. After that, those zombie wanna-bes started hanging out together, started their own thing. After our informative and inspiring article, they got more organized. It's been months and they're still at it."

"Wait." Bob raised his hand.

Rod smacked it down. "Something, for once, is bigger than you."

Bob raised his hand again, this time sweeping the air in front of himself and sending the cloud around him upward. "I don't care about a bunch of cosplay losers."

"You should care." Belmont flicked the lighter. "An object in motion stays in motion with the same speed and in the same direction unless acted upon by an unbalanced force."

Hearing the Newton quote coming from Guy Belmont was no surprise. The wrinkled old man was a constant stream of disturbing reveals. He had been a respected academic, at one time. Long ago. Before he got involved with the tribe. Before he lost his wife and then gradually, slowly, lost his entire life. Hayden studied

Belmont, cigar in one hand, cocktail in the other. He was angled back in the chair, his faded eyes gazing at the wood paneled ceiling. Suddenly, he understood that the two of them had more in common than he'd realized.

"Fine, asshole." Bob shifted, the leather sagging in a new direction as he adjusted himself. "I see your point."

"Do you want to be the unbalanced force? Or let the others be responsible for managing those cosplay losers?"

The door swung open, leaving the question hovering in the air. Elizabeth, still dressed in work clothes, came in, headed directly to the bar. From the hallway, Christopher peered in, scanning the room quickly, before ducking out and closing the door.

"Evening all," she called over, grabbing a wine glass before coming over to take the final empty chair. She unbuttoned her navy jacket then sat. "Pour me some, Hayden," she said, placing the glass on the table. "Please do not tell me what it is. I don't care."

While Hayden poured wine into Hume's glass, a reasonable half full glass for her, Rod hopped off his perch to skip over and kiss her on the forehead. She patted his cheek in return. Rod jogged over to the bar, grabbed another Rolling Rock from the bucket. He twisted off the top and thumbed it across the room. It ricocheted off one of the cage's wood slats, going off at an angle and then landing on its side near the thing. Still upright, it rolled across the floor, coming to a stop when it connected with the burlap lump.

The lump shifted; a hand came out from under the fabric and grabbed the bottle top. The hand and the bottle top both disappeared under the burlap.

"Time for the surprise." Rod scooted away from the bar, returned to his perch on the arm of Bob's chair.

Hayden's stomach clenched. "Can we discuss why we're here?" To hold off the hassle of hard feelings, he added, "No offense, Rod, but I'm not interested in a surprise."

"I'm interested." Elizabeth raised her glass. "It's been a long day. I could use some fun."

Exactly. It had been a long day. But whatever was under that burlap was going to be anything but fun. "Bob," Hayden did his best to hang on to the pleasant smooth tone, "what did you want to discuss?"

Instead of replying, his old boss swirled his glass, staring at the golden liquid. After several long spins, he pointed to the cage. The burlap shifted again, the movement less of a twitch and more of an intentional spin. It was rolling across the floor, kicking against the fabric, probably trying to get free from it. Music pulsed around them, masking sounds with its mechanical rhythm. He'd heard the noises they made when coming to. The creaking, groaning, moaning, and low throated howls were the stuff of nightmares, real and imagined. As long as the music continued drowning out the sounds, he could handle what was enclosed in the cage. He refilled his wine glass and leaned into the soft leather. The others settled back into their respective chairs, each sipping and staring, waiting for whatever Rod insisted was a grand surprise.

The thing continued revolving, and the burlap loosened and fell away, exposing a woman's leg. The limb was short, sturdy, and well-shaped. Her other leg and ass came next. Still partially covered, she rose up on her hands and knees, her naked body slowly convulsing, the waves of tension moving from her bare feet to her bandana-covered head, forcing her to throw her head back each time the wave of electricity passed through her neck. She shook. The rest of the burlap fell away. The bandanna fell off. Ratty shoulder length hair that probably had been shiny back when she'd been human. Now though, the strands were matted in spots.

The smell of her was beginning to drift over, the bitter scent made Hayden's stomach roll. He held his wine glass beneath his nose, swirling it as he breathed in. The spicy fruit drifted through his nostrils, skimmed across the back of his throat, but did not hide the growing stench of the creature becoming animated. He kept the glass there, brushing his lower lip against the cool glass as he watched the thing begin to creep across the floor. Something about the motion tugged on his memory, made his chest constrict. The thing reached the edge of the cage, grabbed the slats and raised its fists one over the other, then used the slats to steady itself into a standing position. Once it was upright, that memory shifted into reality, and he knew. He understood the surprise.

From the cover of his eyes, he looked at each of the others. Elizabeth smirked. Bob's face remained passive, but he nodded, his chin rising and falling with sharp certainty. To him, this was exactly right. The most reasonable thing to happen next. But then, he'd been in on this particular amazement, helped *Roddie* plan it. Belmont's mouth twisted in disgust, disappointment, or both.

The creature propped its small feet on the slats and then, using opposing hands and feet, started to climb upward. Crouching like a crab, it went up the side, reached the top, then dropped its head back, bared its teeth and screeched so loudly the sound cut through the music. Hayden braced himself, grabbing hold of the soft leather. The thing shook its head, tossing its ratty hair in quick sharp turns until, from the corner of its eyes, it spotted them. Then, it, or should he think of it as her, froze.

Had she been a gift from Matthew?

Had one of these demented assholes stolen her?

He looked around the room, studying each face before moving on to the next. No point in raising the question. Truth was not one of this community's core values.

Hayden gave up on masking the horror unfolding before him. He gulped what remained of his wine, set the glass on the table and then, not wanting the others to see how badly this little display was hurting him, set his arms on the armrests and took hold with his trembling fingers. Finally, he forced the tattered remains of his soul deep inside himself, shoving them down so far, he hoped they would never resurface.

"What about now, Hayden?" The flush had returned to Rod's face. He was gleaming with excitement. "Are you interested now?"

Hayden squeezed the arms of the chair harder, and his back sunk deeper into the chair. If only he could force himself through, push through to another dimension, one that wasn't so relentlessly fucked up and cruel.

Rachelle was still clinging to the top of the cage, the skin of her naked body an ashy hue, faded and lifeless and yet… there she was… moving. No longer howling, she moved more quickly, more freely, as though she'd woken up from a nap. But, of course, she hadn't been sleeping. Humans sleep. No human, not even Rod, could contort themselves the way she had. No human could crawl across the top of the cage. Then again, she wasn't human. Not anymore.

"When did you turn her?"

"That's part of the surprise," Bob said.

Rod stood and stretched both of his arms overhead. "We didn't turn her."

"How?" Belmont pointed to the cage, his hand waving up and down as he watched the creature watch them.

"Wouldn't you like to know," Rod replied, bending sideways, his long rib cage pressing against his skin, each bone looking like it could pierce the pale layer.

"As a matter of fact, yes, I would." Belmont turned to Bob, waved his short fingers. "What is this?"

Bob replied without taking his gaze from the cage. "Something Roddie's been working on."

"If she isn't turned, then what is she?"

His gaze moved with the creature. "Don't know exactly." He shrugged. "Somewhere in-between."

The creature's head swiveled. She... it... reached the opposite side of the cage and began skulking down.

"Why? What is the use?"

"A use?" Elizabeth pushed herself to the edge of her chair. Her hands were shaking as she buttoned her jacket. Hayden was sure of it. "Is there a use to any..." her gaze circled the room, taking in the chairs, the Boston sports loaded paraphernalia around the bar, the secret bookshelf that hid the secret hallway that led to the secret room. The playroom filled with disgusting secrets. "...of this?"

Belmont turned his head, his watery gaze shifting to Elizabeth. "Rather late in the game for that line of thinking, isn't it Ms. Hume?"

She set her glass of wine down so sharply red liquid splashed over the rim. "We still on for Sunday night?" She used the arm of the chair to push herself to her feet, teetering on her heels.

"Don't leave, Lizzie." Rod taunted her with an exaggerated pout. "There's more to come."

One of her arms snaked up. She grabbed her elbow. "Not for me, there isn't." She let go, dropped her arm, and then stopped the vibrating of her fingers by fisting her hands. "Sunday night?" She gestured to the cage. "And this is... part of that?"

Bob nodded. Belmont nodded. Hayden's stomach knotted.

"Hayden? You have that list of buildings and locations ready?"

He choked out his reply. "Almost."

"Have it done by tomorrow. We need it for the..." She grimaced as the creature skittered across the floor and started up the side again. "We need it for... we need it. Never mind. Have it ready. Also, I want you to show it to her. She made a promise to help, and I'm going to see that she keeps it."

Bob snorted. "Good luck with that."

"Indeed," echoed Belmont.

Again, Hayden said nothing.

"This is going to go as planned." She paused at the door, turned back to say, "If I have to use the connections, I will."

"She knows damn well what," Bob pointed at the cage, "this is all about. It was her idea we have a way to control... manage them. In case. If—"

"Eradicate." Guy was staring into his empty glass. "I believe that was the word she used."

The music humming around them.

Rachelle's face contorted, her screech silenced by the music, as she moved across the top of the cage.

Chapter Six
"That's part of the surprise."

At 7:30 the next evening, Nidhi's cab pulled up to the curb. Even though she'd tried, the ride to South Boston hadn't given her enough time to get her shit together. She'd been wound up ever since waking up at noon, disoriented and jittery. The dream had been so real, so terrifying that she'd had to examine the front door three times, assuring herself that it had been locked. The downstairs windows, also closed and locked. Even alone in the back seat of the cab, she felt like she was going to throw up. It seemed highly doubtful her body was going to relax any time soon. The best she could hope for would be successfully fake being fine. Or something close to fine.

The car jerked to a stop. "This is the right place?" the cabbie asked over her shoulder.

The building was a far cry from the ones in Beacon Hill. A Rolling Rock sign swung from a single nail. The windows were boarded up, but the place had a door which appeared to be functional. The nail salon to the right had a closed sign hanging in the window. The lot on the other side of the building was covered with the crumpled remains of what appeared to be yet another fallen old building.

"Yeah?" he asked again, louder.

69

Nidhi leaned forward, paid the fare in cash. "Yeah, it is." According to the blue dot on her map, anyway.

The cab rumbled away as soon as she'd closed the door. Outside, she found nothing to assure her she was in the right place. Still, she walked toward the door, following the instructions she'd received from Hume. The text had arrived several hours ago, a simple insistence to meet up even though it was Saturday. That and an additional note instructing her to keep quiet about the meeting. And to come alone. Nidhi had spent the entire afternoon convincing herself the text really was from Elizabeth Hume, not Mattie. Nidhi reached for the chipped chrome handle, but the door swung open before her fingers touched the handle.

"Prompt as always. That's one of the things I like about you."

Elizabeth Hume, smiling, greeting her as though the two of them had arranged to meet for an afternoon of cards instead of a clandestine out-of-the-office off-the-books meeting at a rundown shithole in a bad part of town. Even so, Nidhi was very glad to see it was her overbearing boss holding the door.

"Should I come in?"

The woman pushed the door further open, stepped back.

Nidhi stepped into the dive bar, her Converse sneakers sticking to the ancient, chipped linoleum tile as she followed the woman past the empty tables to a booth in the back. The red vinyl, like everything else, was worn out, stained, torn, and long past used up. Her boss, wearing the odd mix of high heeled boots, high-waisted jeans, and a red cashmere turtleneck, slid right across the tears.

Nidhi pulled off her jacket, tipped sideways to remove her bag then slid in across from her.

"The others should be here any minute. You can get started by reviewing the materials." Hume picked her phone off the table, started scrolling through. Without looking up, she nodded toward the stack of file folders on the table. Some paper news clippings and lined notebook paper stuck out from inside the manila files.

"We're waiting for—oh, here now." She set her phone down, scooted out. She touched the edge of one of the folders. "We have the place to ourselves for now, so relax and enjoy yourself." She strutted to the door, her boots tapping across the tattered floor.

Nidhi flipped back the cover of the file on top. A clipping of Hayden's very first zombie article, the one that started it all. She didn't need to read it. She'd read it a dozen or more times already. Snowmaggeddon. The library. Zombies capturing humans to use them as sex slaves. The absurd Rod McKinon *Zombie Rites* film tie in. And, of course, the reference to Guy Belmont's now famous book, that ridiculous academic text published by a low tier press decades ago. The contents and theories in that very book were the reason he'd faded from the academic scene. Nidhi did not miss the irony of her situation—that text had gotten him banished from the hallowed halls of academia but it, along with the secret one Mattie had told her about, could be her ticket into them.

The tapping of Hume's boots made her look up. Hayden, weaving between the small tables scattered around the room. Given the contents of the file, and that he was now her boss's favorite, him being part of this exclusive, secret meeting was not a surprise. It was annoying.

"Hey Nidhi," he said, his face placid, holding none of the expressions from last night. He dropped onto the seat across the table. Once settled, he added, quietly, "How's it going?"

She pinched her face, wanting to hide the shame and dread clinging from the visions of the night before.

"Everything okay?" Hayden's hands worked down the buttons of his coat, revealing a traditional black, navy and green plaid flannel shirt. Hume was behind the bar, the clank of bottles keeping his voice from carrying.

Nidhi kept her voice low, "Yeah, fine." The news clippings were spread across the table, she used both hands to sweep them into a pile. "Why're you asking?"

"I—I just—"

"I know you like your fancy wines, Hayden," Hume said, cutting him off. "But there is none of that here. Right now, I'm a PBR girl." Elizabeth set four long neck bottles, already opened, on the table then slid in beside Hayden. "And since I'm the boss…" Her laughter ended abruptly in the silence of neither of them joining her.

Hayden twisted out of his coat, then set it on his lap, crossways, the same way he had the night before. Pointing at the bottles, he asked, "Do you want to wait, for—"

"No." Hume grabbed one and took a sip. "We don't need to wait for her." She set the bottle back down and looked at the door. "You can get started filling Nidhi in on what we talked about."

Hayden wrapped his fingers around one of the bottles but didn't drink. "I see you've been looking at the articles."

Nidhi picked up a bottle and looked inside the neck at the golden liquid.

"Have you, um, have you read them?" He took a sip. "Because if you need to read them, we can wait—"

"Yes, Hayden. Of course, I've read them. Even though they won't admit it to you, everyone at the paper has read all of them, too. Fuck, I think everyone in Beantown has read them."

"Hell yeah." Hume smacked the table. "That's the idea."

Nidhi realized then that she'd rarely heard the woman laugh and certainly never that loud.

Once their boss quieted down, he continued. "I left the other articles out for you, Elizabeth. Why didn't you bring them?"

She propped her elbow on the table, rested her chin in her palm, looking at the pages. "I decided those would just confuse the issue. We need to stay focused on the original story." She turned her head to watch the door.

He picked up the very first one he'd written, a clipping from Bob Keeler's *Boston Weekly*, and turned it over. There were some printed out photos on the back. Images of the infamous sex zombie he'd fucked in the library. Hayden glanced at Hume who was still staring at the door, then leaned forward and pointed to the woman on the page. He lifted his eyebrows, tapped the paper, then used his finger to trace an invisible circle around the woman, some crazy bitch he'd talked into dressing up like a trashy zombie Barbie then fuck him on a table right there in the library. The Boston Public Library. The world-famous architectural gem. And all of it, start to finish, on camera, in a video uploaded onto the paper's website. After Bob had edited it, of course.

Hayden stopped moving his hand and glared at her.

She lifted her own brows in question.

He tapped the photo again.

That queasy pull in her stomach returned as she looked over the woman. None of the images had her full body and face in the shot. Each was a piece, an arm and a thigh, a chin, neck and the top of one tit, the top of both tits, covered in the red straps, a thigh showing under the hem of her mini skirt accompanied by the top of her thigh high fishnets. The ends of her hair, side of her neck, her collarbone. The first few times she'd looked at the images, Nidhi had reluctantly accepted that the pieced together style was effective. You never saw the whole zombie, only pieces, sections. You had to use your imagination to pull together all the shots and only then would you know what she looked like. Only then would anyone have a chance at figuring out who she was. Because Nidhi had never given a shit who the mystery woman was, Nidhi had never bothered to stitch the images together.

When she looked back to Hayden, his face was arranged the same as it had been last night. But now, unlike then, she understood. Nidhi's mouth went dry, her guts compacted. No time to ask questions, though, no time to verify because *she'd* come through the door. Instead of the familiar jeans or bike shorts and white T-shirt, she was wearing a skirt. *The* skirt. And fishnets. *The* fishnets. Her hair was down, a mass of tangles framing her face.

Hayden's mouth was flat, his gaze on the two women lingering by the door. Her boss's hands fluttered around her waist, flicking blood red nails so bright they were visible even from a distance. Mattie's hands were in the pockets of her leather jacket, the same coat Hayden mentioned in his descriptions, the same leather jacket that Nidhi herself had pressed her cheek against, breathed in its unique scent. Hume reached forward but didn't touch

Mattie, instead she swung and gestured toward the booth. The two of them pivoted and walked, side by side, across the bar. Seeing her now, in the skirt and fishnets, it was so obvious.

But what did it mean?

Hume slid in next to Hayden, leaving the seat beside Nidhi open.

Mattie stood at the end of the table, put her hands in front, positioning herself as though she was about to take orders instead of give them. "Hey fam."

Throwing up on the table did not seem out of the realm of possibilities. Nidhi concentrated on breathing through her nose, holding her mouth motionless, and willing her body to stay quiet. Calm.

No one spoke.

Hume seemed to suddenly remember that she was, technically, the boss. "Mattie? Do you already know Nidhi?"

"Oh, yes. I'd say we're acquainted." She took her hands from the table and folded her arms across her chest, wrapped in the red bindings so eagerly adopted by the Tribexxers. "We have an, what would we call it, Hayden? An acquaintanceship?" She slid in next to Nidhi, bumping hard against her. "Yes. Yes. I think that's what we have. An acquaintanceship."

Hume picked the bottle she'd already drank from then pointed to the remaining one. "That beer is for you, Mattie"

"Already opened it, Elizabeth? Is it safe? You aren't trying to roofie me, are you?"

Again, Hume laughed, this time less loudly. "Of course not. What sort of woman do you think I am?"

"I know exactly what kind of woman you are. Isn't

that why I'm here?" Mattie picked up the bottle and positioned it above the center of the table, inviting a toast. "To new ventures."

The boss was the first to lift her bottle, Hayden next. Nidhi joined the toast, clinking her bottle and murmuring cheers as her right leg started the shake. Everyone sipped in unison. Swallowed with a grim smile. Like a beer ad. Only without the joy, safe unity, and optimism. The cold liquid moved slowly down Nidhi's throat, chilling her hardened stomach.

Hume lowered her bottle first. "We have about 30 minutes until the performers and crowd start to arrive, so let's get to it."

Hayden took that as a cue to start talking again. He summarized the contents of his articles to date. Mattie and Hume nodded and murmured encouragement and praise, focusing on the one article he'd written with Belmont in particular. That was the last one he'd done for Bob's tabloid before coming to *The Globe.* Occasionally, Nidhi took a sip of the PBR, even though it was something she hated—drinking cheap beer to pretend you were cool, a regular person. None of them were any kind of regular people. Then again, maybe that was the point. A thought that had nagged at her before came screaming back into her mind. Hume was using them. Each one of them and each one for a different reason. Hayden and his shitty articles were her money and, maybe, some taking him on was some sort of repayment to a debt she'd owed to Keeler. Mattie because the girl was willing to do anything. What did that mean for her?

Nidhi's attention returned to the conversation as Elizabeth delivered a bomb. "And so, Belmont is the place, person, to focus on, now."

Belmont? Guy Belmont?

What did he have to do with any of this? With them?

"I haven't talked to him lately." Hayden rubbed his nose, "About any of this." He turned to Hume. "Have you... talked to him about his project?"

She sighed, looking more annoyed than disappointed. "No. He won't talk to me."

"Me either," that from Mattie.

The three of them looked at her, but it was Hume who spoke. "That leaves you, Nidhi. What do you know about him?" She took a sip of her beer, swallowed. They were all staring at her, watching. She scanned the tables, the mis-matched chairs and spotting a couple pink cups far across the room, on the floor under a table by what was once a window.

"What do you know about him?" Hume asked again.

He's an exiled academic who wrote the insane shit that now fuels an entire fandom and microculture which I'm studying and hoping to build my dissertation from. "I've never met him," she said. That was true.

"You haven't done any research on your own?" Mattie asked, her face a mask of curiosity.

Mattie knew for a fact that Nidhi had done research on the man. The other girl had been the one who told her about the pseudonym and the other book. But Mattie had also promised to keep her mouth shut about Nidhi's research on Belmont and the Tribexx fandom. Apparently, the girl was good at keeping her mouth shut about some things because Nidhi had no idea the girl was connected to the paper. When she'd seen her around, she'd just assumed it was because the girl was visiting Hayden.

Fuck. She'd been so stupid.

77

Mattie must've gotten the information about the secret book from Hayden, but up until that meeting, Nidhi hadn't been concerned that Hayden would go looking for that other book. "I thought we—the paper—was done with the zombie stuff."

"Seems the zombies aren't done with us." Again, Hume chuckled at her own joke. "So, Nidhi have you or have you not done any research on Guy Belmont?"

"What kind of research?" she asked.

"Anything." Mattie injected her voice with a girlish innocence. "Anything at all."

"What's the goal here?" Hayden drummed the tabletop. "What are we trying to accomplish?"

Hume and Mattie exchanged glances, their gazes a combination of lingering, assessing, and challenging.

Fuck me.

Another shock rocked through her as Nidhi realized she'd been blinded by lust and ambition. So cliche. How had she not known the two of them had something. Have something. Sexual, secret, twisted, whatever the hell it was she did not want to be part of it. Too late though because she already was.

Hayden continued, "I thought you wanted to ease away from the zombie stuff and focus on historic haunted homes, *the possessions*."

"We think the two are linked." Hume said. "And we want to expose that."

Mattie's face dropped. It happened so suddenly, and she recovered so quickly, it was as though it didn't happen. But it did and Nidhi saw it, and she was ready to use the girl's discomfort to her advantage. "Care to explain?" she asked.

"What if the zombies are using the haunted houses

as cover? They use the abandoned buildings for their dens and explain away whatever people see going on as ghost activity or by saying the house is possessed."

And so, the discomfort was passed to her. Nidhi's parents had been buying vacant properties for a couple years now. They'd started out buying office buildings, then moved on to historic homes and brownstones. They'd been there for her through her bad times—more than she deserved. She owed them protection from whatever bullshit Hume was cooking up. "You know there aren't really any zombies? Haunted houses aren't a real thing."

Hayden sighed. "I thought we were calling them possessed."

"Possessed, haunted, what's the difference?" Hume replied as though they were talking about the weather.

"I think there is a difference," he said.

Nidhi tapped her chin with her finger. "What difference does it make? Neither one is real."

"The public doesn't know that." Elizabeth's tone implied the point of the public's willingness to believe the absurd was the one that mattered most.

If the truth didn't matter, there was only one next logical step. "So… whatever comes from our investigation is not going into *The Globe*."

Hume's barking laughter blended with Mattie's snicker. Hayden glowered. Hume was the one who spoke. "Fuck no."

"It'll be on *the site*?"

Nidhi had heard rumors about a secret site that the paper hosted, a subscription-based website that ran tabloid style articles on scandals and insane shit they could never include in the actual paper. Based on the rumors, the site made money. Nidhi had looked for it, but was never able to find it, but also according to the rumors, it had only been around several months. She looked at Hayden—several months was the same amount of time he'd been at the paper. Apparently, the rumors weren't rumors.

"Of course, on *the site*." Hume continued talking about hits and views and subscriptions, but the words blurred together as she felt her goal for being at the paper crack into pieces. Contributing content to a secret site was not going to help her. Why would she want to be involved? She didn't give a shit about money. She needed publishing credits. And access to information. If anything, writing for the site was going to make her look like a hack, a desperate money-grubbing wanna-be. Why would anyone choose to be involved with the site? Unless, of course, they did not have a choice. Again, she looked at Hayden.

He noticed her staring, and said, "Maybe we should fill Nidhi in on how we work."

Chapter Seven

"Maybe we should fill Nidhi in on how we work."

Hume blinked. "You didn't tell her?"

"No... I—"

"I asked you to fill her in. What were the two of you talking about while I was opening the door for Mattie?"

Nidhi's heart was pounding, her mind buzzing. "He did explain the site," she lied. "But we didn't have time to go into details. Like how this story would fit into the vision."

Hume's face crumbled. "Vision?"

She struggled for a reply. "The long-range plan for the site. Its brand."

"Long range? Good God, I hope not." Hume's sour vibe vanished, replaced by a sardonic smirk. "If they think I'm fucking around with this for the rest of my career they better find a replacement." Her indignance was off, faked. Her anger though, that was real.

Hayden patted the articles. "Elizabeth wants us to use what we have here to generate something new."

"Especially focus on that article Hayden wrote with Belmont. Dig in there and use that as a model." Hume spread her hands, pretending she was discussing something both reasonable and achievable. "Imagine there is an outside body that wants to draw attention *to* some of the abandoned homes and businesses while also drawing attention *away from* other such dwellings. Imagine this outside body wants us to assist in that." She paused, looking at the stack of articles and changing her expression to a mocking sneer. "Or, if it makes you feel better, imagine that improving the condition of these run-down safety hazards will help the less fortunate by making our city a cleaner, healthier, more livable place."

A bomb of silence went off around the table while they each imagined versions of the real, intended scenario. The one that involved assisting some nameless outside body who sought while pretending to be benevolent. Nidhi broke the quiet. "Are you trying to get kids to break into abandoned buildings and look for zombie tribes?"

"Not just kids." Hume snickered as she leaned back, taking a sip from her bottle. "We don't need to bother ourselves with the details. We do the work and get it done. Good things happen next."

Time wasted and time spent away from her actual research. Then again there was the possible connection to Belmont. If this was in fact being done in secret, then her connection to the disgraced academic would also be secret. Her parents wouldn't know she was involved in something that could harm their investments. But if word did get out... Nidhi trusted Hayden to keep his mouth shut, he too had a reputation to build. Mattie though, that girl obviously did not give a shit about what others thought of her and so was a possible threat. "Do I have to work on this?" she asked.

"I wouldn't have invited you here to this ground floor get-together if I didn't think you were right for this special project."

Nidhi set her palm on the tabletop. "I appreciate your confidence, but—"

"You can continue with the little things I've been giving you. Or you can take this opportunity to start doing real writing. Up to you."

Those crap pieces about rich people weren't going to get her parents into trouble. But they wouldn't get her access to Belmont. She leaned back, pulling her palm off the table.

Hume gestured to her golden boy seated beside her. "I thought you were an up-and-comer, like Hayden."

Mattie leaned into Nidhi, her smooth voice a liquid threat. "Want me to get up so you can leave?"

She wasn't even going to bother pretending she had a choice. "No. Thank you," she said to Mattie. Then, to Hume, "Count me in."

"Good." Hume nodded. "No regrets. Plus, like I said, good stuff will happen if this goes the way they... we... want."

Mattie nudged her again, this time under the table with her leg. Was the nudge a flirtation? Or a threat?

"So," Hume started again, "As I was saying, we want to connect the zombies to the haunted houses. We need evidence that this is a real problem."

"Click bait." Hayden leaned back until his head hit the metal Celtics sign nailed to the wall.

Hume pursed her lips. "Evidence."

Hayden continued. "If you want to focus on particular areas, how about a map to the locations?"

Mattie shimmied. "Oh yes, a map. I do love a good map."

"See? I knew you'd be a great addition to this team, Mattie. You and Hayden work on that map together."

Nidhi feigned a casual attitude. "What about Guy Belmont?"

"Are you sure you want to bring that dried up academic into this?" Mattie asked, "What could he possibly have to offer?"

Hayden pointed across the table. "That is Nidhi's job to find out."

Hume tore off a piece of one of the articles, wrote a number on it, and held it out. Nidhi took it, glanced at the numbers then slid it into the pocket of her jeans.

Hume's phone buzzed. She glanced at the screen then stood. Looking at Mattie, she said, "They're outside. You take it from here."

Mattie stood to let Hume scoot out. "Whatever you say."

Hume went to open the door. "I'll be back in a minute." Mattie went the other direction and disappeared behind the bar.

Once she was sure that both were out of earshot, Nidhi whispered to Hayden. "What the fuck is going on?"

He also kept his voice low. "I tried to warn you."

He was not telling her everything. She was sure. "This is more than that."

"I didn't know about this," he pointed to Hume's back then gestured in the direction Mattie had gone. "Until this morning." He scanned the bar top, then skimming the stools dotted with silver duct tape.

Nidhi was a long way from being satisfied. "Did you tell Hume to put me on this?"

After glancing at the door, where Hume still lingered half in and half out, he said, "I don't want to be on it either."

* * *

Forty-five minutes later, Nidhi sat beside Hayden at the bar. Both of them were still waiting for Mattie's return, watching the so-called performers set up, and tipping back fresh PBRs. The files were on the bar top now, in a neat stack positioned between them. Nidhi had already thumbed through all of them and assured Hayden for the third time that she had read everything, looked at all the pictures, and was as ready as she'd ever be for whatever Hume wanted them to do next.

A couple of guys wearing black jeans and black T-shirts had placed a large portable screen in the center of a cleared area in the back and appeared to be hooking it up to a laptop. The possibility of Mattie returning to finish the meeting was looking less and less likely because the bar was apparently open now. Several men had come in alone then sat down alone. Each had a pink plastic cup within easy reach. One had already gone to the bar for a refill, pouring it himself from one of the pitchers that had been left at each end of the bar.

Nidhi nodded to the sparse crowd. "Do you know what they're waiting for?"

Hayden shrugged then started picking at the label on his bottle.

"What is it?" she asked.

"I saw one of these a couple months ago." He glanced over and watched the guys with the computer. "They didn't have a screen or computer though, so I can't be sure it's the same thing."

One of the guys stood back as some industrial techno rumbled from the speakers. It wasn't especially noisy, but it was enough for the bass to make the air hum.

Nidhi tried again, speaking a little louder to get over the music. "Am I going to like it?"

Two women also dressed in all black, came in, joined the others. Hayden looked over, his face blank, as he watched the women unpack boxes they'd brought in. "You're going to wish you never saw it, wish you never knew it happened." He started picking at the label again, adding to the pile of tiny pieces on the bar. "You're going to wish you never came here. Wish you didn't know this place existed."

Seems that Hayden was a believer of his own dark fairy tales because really, how bad could it be. The bar was a public place. There were people, spectators, present. "I thought you didn't know what the performance was going to be."

Still ripping the label off the bottle, he replied, "I don't, not exactly. But I know these… people… and what they're capable of."

More questions would lead to more cryptic replies. The only way she was going to get to the truth was the way she always did—on her own. As the crew in black continued to cut back and forth from the makeshift stage to the outside, more guys wandered into the bar, filled a pink cup, and then found a spot to sit, alone.

Now tearing the pieces of paper he'd piled on the bar, Hayden asked, "You going to call Belmont?"

Nidhi watched another single man settle into a chair, rubbing his long beard in between gulps from the pink cup. "I thought I might text him first. Give him a minute to read my message before he replies. That way he's less likely to be on guard when we talk."

"Don't waste your time texting. He's not what you'd call tech savvy." Hayden watched the two women walk by. One of them carried a brown burlap bag. "Something you should know; the guy isn't as ludicrous as everyone says."

She scoffed. "Oh really?" The man was years deep into his forced retirement from the real world. The only reason anyone knew about him now was because of Hayden's zombie articles. Now the man was some sort of cult hero, sort of like a party favor. Fun and offered a temporary good time but was, in reality, ultimately pointless. "You willing to tell me what you know about him?"

Hayden paused his nervous attack on what had been the beer label and looked toward the door, now swinging open. "Not here."

"When can you meet?"

Hume and Mattie reappeared from behind the bar. Hayden swooped up his pile of tiny pieces and tossed them to the floor. The two women rushed past, walking side by side until parting ways half-way across the room. Hume continued toward the group dressed in black, still working by the screen. Mattie circled back, her hips moving in an exaggerated roll. All the seated men watched the hem of her skirt brush her thighs. No wonder both she and Hayden had fallen for her. She was a lot of things, most of them bad, but also undeniably hot in a dirty, disgusting, chilling way.

Mattie locked gazes with Nidhi as she stepped close. Nidhi flinched. Mattie smiled. Sliding in between them, her back to Hayden, she put her hand on Nidhi's knee. Days ago, the touch would have ignited heat and lust. Now, her response was a mixture of regret and cold fear. There was something else there too. Not lust or desire but something compelling, something pushing her toward the other girl with a cruel unnatural force.

"Wanna see what's downstairs in the dusty old basement?"

Beside them, Hayden was sucking down the remaining half of his beer as though it was the last liquid on earth.

"This building is old. Really, really old." Mattie squeezed Nidhi's knee then glided her hand upward, crushing Nidhi's thigh between her thumb and fingers. "Consider your descent preparation for the articles." That green gleam was back in her eyes, but that was impossible. They were inside. There was nothing nearby to cause a reflection.

Hayden set his now empty beer bottle on the bar with the sharp whack.

"Is it haunted?" Nidhi asked, unsuccessfully pulling her leg from Mattie's grip.

Hayden stumbled off the bar stool and started shoving his arms into the sleeves of his coat.

Mattie watched Hayden as she spoke. "It's something. The trick is, you won't know what until you come see."

All the way in or all the way out. Those were her two choices. She'd just have to keep her guard all the way up. She swallowed the last of her beer, set the bottle down, then hopped off the stool. She put on her jacket and her bag. Mattie wrapped her arms around Nidhi's waist and the two of them walked off without saying goodbye to Hayden.

Mattie guided her around the bar, through a storage room that doubled as an office, to a scarred, old door made of several layers of wood. It was loaded down with three large locks. She tapped each of the locks with her fingertip. "Makes you think there's something naughty in there, doesn't it?" She glanced over, her mouth pulling into what could pass for a smile.

Now Nidhi knew her imagination was playing with her mind. Eyes did not change color. "Naughty or illegal?"

Mattie lifted one of the locks then worked the combination dial on the bottom. "Which would you prefer?"

"Interesting."

The other girl continued working, spinning and releasing the locks one at a time. Once the third was open, she set all three locks on a small shelf beside the doorway, then stepped back to pull the door toward her. "We have interesting covered, so you won't be disappointed." She moved through the doorway, then stepped back to let Nidhi pass. She pointed to the bottom of the stairs. "Wait there."

As Nidhi started down, the sound of locks clicking into place came from behind. Back over her shoulder, she saw Mattie using the last of the three combination locks to seal the door from the other side. A warning shiver rattled her spine as she looked from the padlocks and focused on the descent. Each step took her deeper into a cool darkness that included a slightly familiar, bitter smell. The scent intensified, settling in the back of her throat. She tried to identify it, but the efforts only amplified the confusion and created in her a sense of disgust so intense it bordered on revulsion. Behind her, the thump of Mattie's boots came in a quick rhythm.

Nidhi paused on the last step, eyeing the packed dirt floor. Cold air carried both the odd smell and another scent, the second one raw and earthy.

"Left, right, or straight ahead. Go whichever way you like."

"Which is most interesting?"

"Hard to say, baby. Each is different. Each is interesting in its own way."

Nidhi turned left, walking slowly to let her eyes adapt to the low light. There was no adjusting to the smell. She moved deeper in, saw some burlap bags lying on the floor, one beside the other. Mattie brushed past her and took something from the wall. Seconds later, a torch illuminated the area, making all the bags covering the ground visible. Nidhi tried to count them, but there were too many, and they extended beyond the edges of the light.

The temperature had gone up. Perhaps they were moving toward the furnace.

"Keep going."

Mattie was behind her, holding the torch high, giving them a path of light to walk into.

Further down, a wooden shelf blocked part of the view beyond. On it were piled more long burlap bags. Three steps later, she stood before the first in a row of shelves. She set her fingers on one of the bags. Forty-nine was written near the end seam. Beside that bag was number 50. Above, 123. Below 13.

"Interested yet?"

The question was simply bait. Nidhi continued along the rows, scanning the numbers, noting differences in the handwriting. Some numbers were faded. Others looked fresh, as though they had been left on the burlap just days ago. "Hold the torch higher," she said.

Mattie lifted it.

Nidhi's stomach rolled, sending bile up her throat. "How far back do they go?"

"What you want to know is how many are there."

Nidhi took a step back, considering. "How many of what?"

"Open one. Look for yourself."

Nidhi went to the end of one of the racks, put her fingers on a bag labeled 32. She put her palms on the fabric and pressed down. Hard, like dried meat. She moved her hand down the length of the bag. The size of the contents shifted but the texture remained the same.

"What is this place? Some kind of doomsday bunker? Somebody waiting for the end of the world?"

"That sounds judgmental, Nidhi. I thought you academics were more accepting."

Nidhi moved her hands further along the bag, the large size gave way to something smaller, round. Her chest heaved. Her mind went black. But her hands continued to move, going up to the top where the bag was pulled shut with a drawstring. Using both hands now, she loosened the string, opened the top. She spread the opening wide, then guided it downward, revealing what looked like deep brown human hair. She pulled the opening further down.

It was human hair.

Beneath the hairline was a pair of vacant human eyes, lower a nose. The lips were chapped, slightly apart, pulled back in a grimace. White teeth and a gray tongue visible inside. There were eight bags on the rack in front of her. There were more racks all around, an uncountable number of racks holding an uncountable number of bags.

Not bags.

Bodies.

Nidhi let go of the burlap and spun, her gaze connecting with Mattie's green gleaming eyes.

Mattie's mouth pulled into a cruel smile. "Starting to understand? Finally?"

"I—I..." It wasn't possible. It couldn't be true.

Nidhi's chest heaved, pulling in the bitter scent. Her gaze darted, everywhere she looked, bags—more bags.

Bodies.

More bodies.

Mattie grabbed Nidhi's waist, pushed her backward against the wall. She pinned her arms to the side of one of the shelves. "For such a smart girl you really are quite dumb."

Humans.

So many humans.

All around them.

Dead and not dead.

"Dormants." The word came out as a whisper.

"That's right, baby." Mattie started taking off Nidhi's jacket. It hit the dirt floor in a soft thump. Next, she pulled up her sweater, pawed at her breasts covered by a red lace bra. "Not you though. You're alive."

Mattie continued grabbing at Nidhi's breasts, watching her own strong fingers digging under the lace to squeeze the soft, yielding flesh. The harsh motions obviously not meant to seduce or arouse but instead a threat for her to stay still. Give in. Again. Another reality hit hard. Last night wasn't a dream.

"I thought…" She grabbed at Mattie's hands.

The other girl brushed them away. "You thought a lot of things, surprise—you thought wrong."

Nidhi scanned her mind, scrolling through the facts she remembered from Hayden's articles, looking for a way to deny the truth surrounding her. "But the camp…"

"The camp was only temporary, a little break from the city. A private place for us to stretch out and enjoy the winter." She lifted her head. "This is us, though, right here in this basement." With a purr that came across as a threatening growl, she began pawing at Nidhi's breasts again. "You aren't afraid, are you?"

Frozen from the impossibility of it all, Nidhi squeezed her eyes closed.

"You aren't in danger here." Mattie leaned in and ran her tongue down the side of Nidhi's face. "If I wanted to hurt you, you would already be hurt." She moved over to lick the other side. "As it turns out, I don't want to hurt you. I like you." After another threatening purr, she added, "You like me too. Otherwise..." She left the sentence unfinished, but the meaning was clear. *Look what you've already done with me? You've already said yes.*

And so, there she was. Face to face, body to body.

The rough grabs of the other girl's hands did nothing to excite Nidhi. Not this time. Pieces of information and memories fell into place, the truth so dreadful her brain continued to seek other explanations. Because it couldn't be true. It couldn't possibly be true. None of it. But it was. And she was there, locked in the basement with this, this... thing, holding her captive.

Possessing her.

And the Tribexxers thought it was all a game, the darkest of all let's pretend.

Mattie slowed her attack, her gaze swinging side to side, taking it all in. "This is part of our forever home. This cozy basement is a maze of tunnels and underground rooms." The punishing motion of her hands stopped. "Maybe parts of it are left over from Prohibition. Maybe parts of it were clandestine meeting places for the colonists. We've been using it and will be using it. It belongs to us, and we belong to it."

"For how long?" Nidhi tried to see the end of the rows but could not. How many bodies? How many lives on hold?

Mattie chuckled. "This one place? Decades. Maybe longer. I'm not a historian. Neither are you. So, who cares?"

I care.

"This one place?" she said, wanting some fact, some piece of the truth. "There are more places?"

Mattie unhooked Nidhi's bra. Once the lace was loosened, she sucked on her nipples, flicking the tips with her cool tongue, sucking and flicking, occasionally looking up at her with those green glazed eyes. Nidhi's entire body was locked in fear. Not even her fingers trembled.

There had to be a way for her to wake her own nerves. To get some small sense of herself back. Move. But what good would it do? Shove Mattie? She'd be outpowered in an instant. And where would she run? Into the sea of bodies? Up the stairs to the locked door?

Trying to avoid the overwhelming stench, Nidhi opened her mouth to breathe. The scent quickly coated her tongue, settled in the back of her throat, a bitter pill she'd never be able to swallow. She stared at the cobweb covered rafters. Mattie left her breasts and moved lower, grazing her lips down over her stomach, stopping at the top of her jeans. Seconds later, the button was undone, the zipper down. The pants lower, lower still until the pant legs were puddled around her ankles, like a hobble.

The thin piece of lace between her legs went quickly when Mattie grabbed it and yanked. Mattie knelt, then looked up, that same cruel smile pulling on those full lips Nidhi had thought so sly and sexy only 24 hours ago. The smile fell away then Mattie turned her head down and pressed her mouth to the line of curls covering Nidhi's pussy.

Chapter Eight

"You're going to wish you never came here."

"They'll be waiting. Bring her to the cage."

Nidhi forced her eyes open.

A man, naked except for a pair of black leather chaps slung low on his hips, strolled through the racks, coming toward them. With his tattooed biceps and shaved head, he could pass for a Goth fantasy boy toy, but his lean face held no captivating mystery. He gripped a battered tin mug in his outstretched hand. He was looking at her, willing her to speak with his black gaze.

There were no words in her, though. Only a haze of terror and confusion. She had no intuition to tap into. There was only the stench in her mouth and the wet fear holding her body so tight she couldn't even shiver.

He held up the mug. "You'll be wanting this, Nidhi."

Her name from his mouth, another threat. She would do as she was told. Or end up with her face covered, her body not yet dead, left on a shelf for years. For decades. Only seen again when the tribe decided to turn her, bring her into their group of sexual monsters that fed from humanity, stole the most intimate parts of a person and used them to sustain their cruel lifestyle.

"She's my pet. I decide what she wants and what she doesn't."

Mattie released Nidhi, stepping over to take the mug from the man. Nidhi adjusted her clothes, covering her body, hiding the shame of letting the other woman touch her, use her, that way. Mattie turned, waving the mug in the direction of the man's naked ass, shifting as he walked back in the direction from which he'd come.

"That's Matthew."

Mattie grabbed Nidhi's shoulders and pulled her forward. When they reached the bottom of the stairs, Nidhi looked left. If they had been in the stacks, and were headed to the cage, what horrors lie in wait down that hall?

They all continued forward, eventually passing between two men wearing fur cloaks. The walls changed from concrete to stone, the same sort of stone on her very own Acorn Street. The cozy, idyllic street that dozens of tourists strolled across each day, snapping selfies, and admiring the historic perfection. The picture-perfect place she'd been stupidly bored with the day before. It was now a world away and she desperately wished to be there in her too fancy, too expensive home.

They arrived at a transition marked by a frame of boards. A bright blue tarp hung down, covering the opening. Matthew swept the covering to the side, held it as she and then Mattie passed through. Beyond, was a bed, piled with pillows, a cabinet, and a gold velvet wing back chair. Bundles of dried herbs hung on the stone walls. In front of the chair was a low table covered with various sizes of mugs. It wasn't the mugs, though that snagged Nidhi's interest. It was the jars. Some were short and round, but most were long, shaped like test tubes.

And then there was the cage.

Matthew dropped himself into the velvet chair. The lit candles positioned around the room made the wood slats of the cage glow warmly, but the open door looked anything but inviting. The structure looked like exactly what it was, a confinement for torture. Just as Hayden had described in the articles.

"Does it look as you expected?"

Mattie came up behind her. She snaked her arm around Nidhi's waist, pulling her back until their bodies merged. The other girl reached forward, lifting the mug as she indicated the top of the cage. A webcam was clamped to the top rail.

"Time for the show," Matthew said as he wrapped his fingers around his cock.

"Don't worry pet," Mattie murmured, pushing Nidhi toward the open door of the cage. "No recording devices are allowed. So when we're done, it'll be like it never happened."

Nidhi stiffened. Mattie held the mug aloft as she shoved harder, forcing Nidhi into the cage. Once they were inside, Matthew rose, holding his dick with one hand as he locked the door with the other. Mattie set the mug on the ground by the door.

"I have to make sure everything is ready upstairs." He leaned close, candlelight blinking off the row of rings pierced into the side of his hear. "No fucking until I get back." The thud of his feet faded quickly.

"What is it you want from me?" Nidhi stepped around the black rug, thick with fur, laid out in the center of the cage floor.

"I want the same thing you want." Mattie threw off her leather, then crept after her, following her around the small area.

Nidhi scanned the murky corners of her mind. Came up empty.

"Don't overthink it." Mattie said, cupping her breasts with her palms, then dropping them after pinching her nipples through the red strips of fabric.

Nidhi grabbed the door and tested the lock. Of course, it was secure. "I want out of here."

Mattie pointed to the camera. "You're going to get out, once you give me what I need." She ran her tongue across her top lip. "Then you're going to get me what I want."

"Are you going to kill me?"

"Don't be stupid." Mattie smirked, beginning to undo her skirt. "If I do that, I won't be able to use you."

"Use me for what?"

The skirt fell to the floor, exposing Mattie's bare pussy. "Weren't you concentrating during the meeting?" The thigh high fishnets and boots were still on. The vision of her muscular thighs flexing as she strode was fierce and feral. "Didn't you write down your one to-do item? What sort of professional are you going to be if you don't take notes and do as you're told?"

Nidhi paused in the corner opposite the entrance, braced herself against the wooden bars. "Belmont?"

"Yeah." Mattie twisted her lips together as she tucked her hands between her legs. "Belmont."

Nidhi came out of the corner, paced, looking for something, anything that she might use to her advantage. "Go find him yourself."

"I can find him. I can't get him to talk to me. I don't feel like fucking the information out of the old, wrinkled bag of sticks." Mattie braced herself in the opposite corner and looked her over with those green glowing eyes. "Anyway, I'll be too busy fucking you." She loosened the straps binding her breasts.

Mattie had been the one who told her about Belmont's secret pen name, that he'd written another book and had information that he'd withheld from Hayden and all the weirdos who interviewed him after the articles made him temporarily famous. But why could she possibly care about what he had hidden from the world? "What—"

"Show time."

Mattie pointed up. "Watch for the light, pet. That's how you'll know it's go time."

Eyes focused on the camera; Nidhi backed herself into the corner. Matthew sat in the velvet chair, started humming. Or was it a chant?

The light blinked blue.

Mattie left, grabbed the top of the cage then swung forward and let go. She grabbed Nidhi on the way down, taking them both to the ground. They landed on the rug with Nidhi's face buried in the black fur, the remaining binding straps coming undone, a ribbon of red around them. Mattie was on top of her, rolling her over then pinning her. The green flash in her eyes was bright now, luminous.

"Now is the time to decide." Mattie guided her nipples across Nidhi's cheeks, then kissed her forehead. A dense chill shook Nidhi's skull, the vibration so sudden it made her ears ring. "Tea or no tea? Memory?" She set one breast over Nidhi's mouth. "Or no memory?"

The light above blinked.

"They can see but can't hear. So don't bother calling for a hero."

"They paid money for this, pet." Matthew, still caressing his cock, leered over at them. "None of those assholes would want to come down here and save you.

99

Unless, of course, they could get in there with you instead."

"Is that what you'd like? One of them instead?" Mattie sat back on her heels, spreading her thighs, exposing all of her bare pussy. "We could make some money on it."

"Do an auction." Matthew said. "Practice for tomorrow."

"That's right," she said, opening and closing her legs. "Matthew could go up those stairs and find out who's the highest bidder."

Matthew laughed, the sound more like the bark of a hyena than any human laugh she'd ever heard. "It'll be the worst, most disgusting, vile loser in the bunch."

She bent down and smacked her ass. "This is what they do on a Saturday night. They're all vile." Mattie raised her hand, then lifted her middle finger. "It'll be the one with the most money."

Matthew laughed louder, the sound ending in a snort. "It'll be the one who has the nerve to come down here and do it."

"We could split the money with you." Mattie poked Nidhi's stomach. "But you don't need money? Do you, rich girl?"

Nidhi tried to get off her back. Mattie slid her hand under the waistband of her jeans, held her in place, and asked, "What's it going to be?"

Nidhi's lips started to quiver. Her legs started to shake.

"I want to hear you say it. Out loud." Mattie, still holding on to her pants, lifting her off the ground as she got to her feet. "Say, I want you, Mattie. I want you to fuck me until I like it."

Nidhi's limbs swung through the air, her hands grasping nothing.

"You can say it for me." Mattie dropped her, and she hit the rug with a hard thud. "Or one of them."

Nidhi disregarded the pain in her mouth from biting her tongue as she scrambled to her feet, took hold of the bars to stop herself from wobbling.

"We can use some extra cash." That from Matthew, his voice mocking.

Nidhi tasted blood as she sucked in a gulp of air then forced the words out. "I want you, Mattie."

"And?"

Nidhi blocked out her heart, closed off her body and went all the way in, diving deep into their black pool, going lower, finding the bottom. She squatted. "Fuck me until I like it."

Mattie dropped herself to the floor and cupped her breasts, lifting them playfully for Nidhi. "Take off your clothes."

There were two ways she could play it. Scared, unwilling. That's what they wanted.

She'd go the other way.

She lifted her chin, looking away from Mattie and seeking the camera lens. Forget the ratty room above her, block out the sad, single men who'd paid to see her hurt and humiliated. Imagine another world. One where she alone made her decisions, and she alone guided her desire. After kicking off her ankle boots, she reached down and unbuttoned her jeans. Next, she lowered the zipper, slowly, link by link. Once her jeans were open, she rolled onto her back, shoved her palms under the fabric, raised her hips, sliding the material lower, onto her thighs. She lifted her knees, shoved the material down, wiggling her ass as she finished pulling the pants off. After she tossed the pants aside, she curled her knees to her chest, then slid her hand between her legs and began caressing herself, running her fingertips over the black lace thong.

Mattie glared at her, one hand on her bare hip. "All of a sudden, you've turned into a sex kitten?"

"I've always been a sex kitten." Mimicking Mattie, she slid her hands under her bra and cupped her breasts. "If you hadn't been such a manipulative bitch you would've gotten to find that out in a nicer way." She pulled her hands away and adjusted the bra back into place.

Mattie leaned over her, blocking the camera's view of Nidhi small scale sex show. "Like I give a shit about that."

So, the tough zombie babe had a weak spot. "I think you do give a shit." Nidhi stretched her left leg and set her toes on Mattie's knee. "Now that I know who… what… you are, I'm not ever, ever going to like you the way you want me to."

Matthew groaned, then shouted, "Shut the fuck up."

Nidhi wasn't surprised that he was losing his patience. There couldn't be much worse than dealing with a roomful of pathetic Incels, all whining about the girls not getting it on fast enough and also to their liking. "Afraid of the crowd losing interest, Matthew?" she said.

"Did you tell her she could talk to me?"

Mattie pushed Nidhi's toes from her knee. "Don't talk to him."

"Why, you both worried the losers up there will start a riot? Mess the place up?"

"You don't know what you're doing." Mattie took

Nidhi's foot and squeezed, mashing her toes together. "Acting up will make things worse."

"I don't see how things could get any worse." She jerked her foot away.

"That's the problem. You don't know what you don't know."

Nidhi rolled onto her side, flipped onto her hands and knees, crawled to the opposite side of the cage, then stood. Standing there in only her bra and thong, she watched Mattie, coming slowly toward her. The green glowing eyes a flicker of hideous light. "Let's get this over with," she said.

Mattie leaned in, her voice a hot whisper. "I'm not trying to scare you. I'm trying to protect you."

They stood toe to toe. Mattie's face inches above.

"Bit late for that, isn't it?" Nidhi whispered back.

A sharp knock came from behind. Matthew, rapping on the wood slats.

Mattie said, more loudly, "We need to give them a show."

"That's right, pet." Matthew emphasized his words with sharp raps on the wood. "We all want a show."

Mattie snagged one of Nidhi's bra straps and yanked, pulling the cup down until one breast was exposed. She went after the other side and did the same. Nidhi didn't fight. She didn't act up. She simply stood still, bracing for what was next.

"Get the tea."

Matthew held the mug through the slats. Mattie took it, held it aloft, into the camera's eye. She was looking at the webcam too, her glowing eyes becoming more vibrant, her body more tense, more threatening.

She lowered the mug, held it under Nidhi's chin.

Stints in rehab, her mother's support, her own tears and promises. Never again, she'd said. But now, Nidhi opened her mouth, swallowed the bitter liquid, and welcomed whatever oblivion would follow. The mug hit the floor with a rattle, the remaining portion rippled across the floor, quickly being absorbed into the dirt.

Matthew returned to the chair. His lips pulled back, showing his teeth as he stroked himself, murmuring, "That's more like it."

Mattie tugged the bra straps down until they snagged on Nidhi's elbows, then yanked the fabric from behind. The binding wasn't necessary. The tea had already begun to take effect. It wasn't the same as the night before. There was no dense fog of mindlessness, no hazy distorted perceptions. The high wasn't like anything she'd ever experienced. It was a stirring of her own nature, the nasty parts of herself she'd quieted and tucked away. Parts she didn't want. Parts nobody wanted. They were the culmination of everything evil that had been done to her—intended and not—there in her soul, making her want to do the same.

Express the pain. Let it out.

Use it.

Nidhi arched her back, shoved her tits in Mattie's face. The other girl took one breast in her hand, squeezed roughly, turning the soft skin one way then the other. Nidhi winced but didn't pull away. Instead, she welcomed the pain and fed from it, used the hurt as though she'd inflicted it on herself. In a way she had. She hadn't listened to the warnings. She'd moved ahead even when her intuition told her that a shitstorm waited for her.

"That's more like it," Matthew encouraged from his chair.

Now, Nidhi struggled against the bind of the bra. Her efforts didn't free her arms, but she found that she liked the constraint. She had an excuse to not fight back, to let Mattie continue the assault. And she did continue taking. She moved her hand to the other breast, grabbing, twisting, pulling. Consuming. Feeding.

Nidhi's head dropped back, her mouth open. She was vaguely aware of the light, continuing to glow above them. She was also vaguely aware of the draw of this, this sexual flight. As Mattie fed from the blackness inside her, pulling the grim memories and emotions through her veins, removing them. Or giving them a life of their own. Nidhi was vibrating. Electric. Buzzing in a new, terrible, way.

Mattie slid her hand between Nidhi's legs, giving her clit the smallest, most gentle caress. "Tell me something about yourself."

Nidhi arched her back and turned. Squeezed her eyes shut.

"Tell me." The other girl lifted her hand. "Or I'll stop."

Nidhi wanted this cruelty. She took comfort in its familiar embrace.

"I—I…"

Mattie replaced her hand, applied enough pressure to tease. "Go ahead. Tell me about the research."

"I'm using it for… a paper." The end of her new beginning, pages of words, ideas, and truths, which would make all her dreams come true. "It'll eventually be…" again she stalled, wanting so badly to fall back into the grim abyss where her responsibilities ceased to exist.

"Eventually what…" The caresses continued, the flickers bringing a new life into her body, distracting her from the reality of her situation.

Eventually she would be free from working under the thumbs of others. She would be the one in control of her life. Her own success, achieved by her own doing. "Dissertation."

Mattie's hand moved to her waist. Fingers spread wide. The touch an easy stroke at first but turning into another grab as her fingers dug into the lower end of Nidhi's ribcage. The malicious touch didn't feel bad. It made sense. It was her punishment. A cleansing. Give in. Take it. Accept. Nidhi closed her eyes, blocked out the camera and the men above.

This was a time for her alone. Her time to rid herself of errors and carve her way into the future. She'd finally be free of the guilt from wasting her privileged, perfect upbringing.

"I know that. Everyone knows that." Mattie softened her grip. "Tell me something I don't know. Something nobody knows."

What could there possibly be?

"There's nothing." Nidhi frowned at that sad truth. "I'm not... interesting."

"Tell me what you're hiding."

A secret? Yes, she had secrets Everyone did. Yesterday, the bed, the wine, the sex. That was a secret. There was something else, she fought the haze, fought against the gratifying humiliation of Mattie's touch. Her kitchen counter. The door. Talking to Easton.

Mattie stopped the assault, released the tension on the bra. The garment fell to the floor. "Want me to tell you something about myself?"

Nidhi tried to think, but her mind was numb. Her entire body was vibrating. She could be floating or buried deep in the earth. Aching for more of the assault, she groaned. "Yes," she whispered. "Tell me."

"Matthew is my brother." Mattie guided Nidhi down, lowering her until the two of them were seated on the black fur rug. "That's how much I mean to him."

"Why…"

"He's why I'm here."

"No… no why… why does it matter…"

The fur brushed against Nidhi's ass cheeks. Mattie continued to lower her onto her back.

"He never wants to be alone."

Nidhi squirmed, wriggling her hips to make the most of Mattie's constant touch.

Suddenly, the touch stopped and Nidhi focused solely on Mattie's voice. "Remember that. He won't ever be alone. He won't allow it."

Nidhi ached for more of the voice, the vibration of it, the satisfying hurt it delivered. "What… what do you want?"

Mattie grunted as she pushed on Nidhi's forehead, and she sagged onto the fur. Seeing the light above nudged her memory. Something. Someone. Not someone. Many.

"I'm the star of this show." She stared at the light, imagining that she could feel all the eyes on her.

Mattie was wrapping something around her ankles. "That's right, you are. Isn't that magical?"

The center of it all. "It is."

"This next bit is just for show, baby. The assholes like to see the ropes. Don't be scared. These ones are nice and long. Lots a space to play." Mattie moved to the opposite side of the cage and started tying the rope to one of the wooden slats. "Don't you feel so good about yourself?"

Mattie crossed the cage and secured the end of the

other rope. Nidhi's leg moved, sliding outward, spreading her thighs in opposite directions.

"Yes." She raised her shoulders and spread her arms. "I'm a star. The star. And I'm going to give you what you need."

Nidhi lifted her hips, buzzing from the counter tension of the ropes. "Oh yeah." What was it that she wanted for herself? Mattie didn't have it, though. Whatever it was. All that was down here were the sad dormant bodies of people who used to be human. And her own detestable nature.

Perhaps that was what she wanted for herself. The chance to let this disgraceful part of herself free.

"There's a price."

She frowned. "How can I pay? I am the money."

"Tell me something no one else knows." Mattie touched Nidhi's thighs, her hands moving lightly across the soft flesh. "About you."

"I..." Nidhi's eyes drifted shut. Nothing. She didn't have any secrets that she hadn't already told Mattie. Well, except the one. She opened her eyes. The other girl squatted between her legs. She lifted her hips again, moaning, begging with her eyes for the other girl to taste her. Eat her pussy. Make her fight against the pleasure.

Ask me again tomorrow, she wanted to say.

It was too late; Mattie's mouth was already on her. Matthew was there too, coming in through the door, then passing the rug. He knelt above her, then rolled her forward, forcing her face onto her knees. He continued pushing until her ass lifted, then shoved her forward until she toppled over.

"Hands and knees," he said.

She scrambled. The ropes tugged on her ankles.

Once she got herself to her hands and knees, she was rewarded with Matthew's dick in her face. Mattie crawled in from behind, finding her pussy again, eating her out like the hungry thing she was.

Matthew lifted Nidhi's chin, pried her mouth open and shoved the tip of his cock between her lips. "Lick it, bitch."

She did, stroking the tip with the end of her tongue, doing her best to show him she could be obedient and earn his trust and affection.

"That's right. Be a good girl and I'll give you more."

She murmured her agreement and continued licking. Soon she was mimicking Mattie's rhythm, matching the surreal strokes and enjoying it. Matthew took a fistful of her hair and thrust more of his cock into her mouth. She opened wider. Her muscles sagged, the last of her will evaporated. She willed him to thrust in.

He did.

She gagged.

The three of them became one.

Her own self evaporated, floated up above the cage, above the crowd of depraved men, and above the old building. She drifted into the clouds, only her physical body remained. But she wasn't alone. It was the three of them together, twisting, thrusting, and becoming something new.

Chapter Nine
"Be a good girl and I'll give you more."

"Come back to us, Nidhi."

Nidhi fought through the hungry haze in her mind.

"It's time for another act."

The dread and fear she'd forced deep down inside herself began to break loose. Without the tea, she had no way to control it, to get beyond it. She curled into herself, wrapped her arms around her legs and squeezed herself into a small knot. Pieces of the memory found her, shamed her, showed her parts of herself she longed to deny. Mattie stood outside the cage by the door.

Nidhi turned, looking instead at the back of the cage.

"I know what you're thinking, baby."

Back when they'd first met, the nickname had sounded sexy. Special. Now, she realized, that was part of the ploy. The game to draw her in, disarm her. "Don't call me that."

"Have I hurt your feelings?" she asked, dipping one shoulder.

Feelings. Feelings?

"What more are you going to do to me?"

The latch thumped. The hinges squeaked. "Depends. What are you going to do for me?"

"Your fucked up live stream isn't enough?"

"That was just some fun. Well, yeah, we did need to make some cash. So—thanks for that." Mattie laughed, the sound mocking and sinister. "Don't you remember me telling you I wanted to go on a trip?"

Nidhi winced. "Yeah. And we did."

Mattie stayed outside the cage, holding the door open. "Oh no, baby. That was just the start."

Nidhi rolled over, bringing the rug with her to cover her naked body. "Just tell me what the fuck you want."

"Isn't this way so much more fun?"

"You're being a pathetic bitch; you know that, right?" The camera light was off. Matthew gone.

"Oh no. Am I taking feminism back a few years? You're already sad that no one will give a shit about your fucked up MeToo story?"

Nidhi began untying the ropes from around her ankles. When Mattie made no move to stop her, she completed the task then gathered her clothes. "You're going to let me walk out of here? No new torture plan?"

"It didn't seem like torture to me. You'll be ready for more when the time comes."

She adjusted her bra. "Getting a bit ahead of yourself, aren't you?"

"Oh no, not at all. Why don't you ask Hayden? He'll tell you about the *torture*."

Nidhi got to her feet and pulled on her jeans. Once they were zipped, she grabbed her sweater, pulled it on.

"You have that little chore on your to-do list."

"What the fuck are you talking about."

"Belmont." Mattie sneered. "Have you forgotten already?"

She found a hair band in the pocket and used it to make a ponytail. "What the fuck do you care about him?"

She waved to indicate their surroundings. "Seems kinda obvious now, doesn't it?"

No. It did not seem obvious at all. But she wasn't going to try a different angle. There would simply be another barb, another contest that she would again lose. She brushed past Mattie and went to the steps. The other girl came along behind, then shoved past her and started up the steps. At the top, she lifted the first lock, began working the combination. Soon, the door was open, Mattie on the other side, reaching for the strap of Nidhi's bag. For a brief second Nidhi hung at the top of the stairs, until Mattie tugged her forward, throwing her onto the floor. Scrambling, Nidhi got her legs underneath herself.

Mattie ducked back behind the door, the click of the first lock audible from the other side. Nidhi imagined the other girl sliding the two additional locks into place then descending into the catacomb of bodies.

The smell of stale beer and sweat lingered in the empty bar. The screen was gone, the monitors and the disgusting assholes who'd watched her degrade herself, also gone. The Sam Adams beer clock indicated noon. No one, except Easton, would be wondering where she was. She pulled out her phone, requested an Uber, then went outside to wait in the drizzly Sunday morning.

* * *

The driver pulled up in front of the office building. After mumbling her thanks, Nidhi tumbled out. Inside, the halls were quiet, the elevator empty. Elizabeth's office was vacant. Knowing that Hume, like other old people, still printed the internet, Nidhi went to the collaborative space she shared with Hayden and the others and went straight for the one printer in the office. The tray was empty, but she got lucky when she dug down to the bottom of the trash. She tucked a single page into her pocket then pulled out her phone. Guy Belmont answered on the second ring.

"I've been expecting your call," he said.

She paused. "Oh."

"Did you have a nice time yesterday?"

"I—I—"

"The meeting with Elizabeth and Hayden?"

Why did everyone keep saying the old man was a clueless washed-up loser when that obviously wasn't true. Everyone except Hayden, anyway. "You mean the one at...that bar?"

"Yes, of course. The Southie. And Mattie was there." He coughed, then came back. "Did you? Did you have a nice time?"

Her, on her back, squirming under the camera. Mattie, throwing her to the ground, pinning her. Matthew watching. All of the others, watching as the tea took effect, brought out that buried side of her. The humiliation and shame felt like a coating on her skin, a weight on her soul. "A nice time? I wouldn't say that, no."

"You saw the basement."

She sat on the desk. "Yes. I did."

A pause, then, "That must have been unpleasant." For a beat she thought he was going to say I'm sorry. But when he spoke again, his voice had already lost the tiny hint of gentleness. "Your experience will make our conversation easier, though. Imagine if I had to convince you that the rumors were true. And then explain the rest."

She should have seen this coming, Belmont knowing more than she did. Mattie knew about Belmont's book and the article Hayden did with Belmont.

These people were all connected. She should've seen that coming, too.

Did Bob Keeler, the man who put the article in his paper know the truth?

And then she realized—"Hume? Elizabeth Hume..."

"Yes, naturally she knows the truth about the tribe." He responded to the murmur of a woman before asking her, "You didn't know?"

Nidhi spun around, away from the walls of the office. Outside, for the first time in days, the sun sliced through the clouds, illuminating the sky to a combination of fluffy white clouds and bright blue. "I'm just now getting it."

"That must be very disturbing."

She stared at the blurry orange sun. "To say the least."

"We should meet. Now." He mumbled something incoherent to someone else, then said to Nidhi, "You know the Dunkin Donuts on the corner by the office? Your paper's office. Meet me there."

"When?" She adjusted the strap of her bag, scooted off the desk, then headed toward the door.

"Don't know how soon. I'll start with the shoes and be there when I get there." He clicked off.

* * *

Nidhi was on her second medium coffee with extra cream when the old man came in. He went to the counter, placed an order, then waited there until he was handed his bag and cup of coffee. Hands full, he acknowledged her. as he sat down in the seat across from her. He wasn't what she'd expected. The articles and blog posts always described him in such a condescending but vivid way that what she saw was, in a way, a letdown. Instead of a quirky eccentric character, he was simply a basic old man. His face was wrinkled, he sat lightly bent over, still wearing his beige coat. Although she hadn't looked, she was certain he was wearing some sturdy brown shoes.

Once settled, he pulled a chocolate frosted donut from the bag and took slow measured bites and patting his weathered lips in between each one. He paused at the halfway point. "Tell me what you know. Not what you've been through. No, not that. What you *know*."

While he ate, she told him the minimum, leaving out as much of herself as possible. She said nothing about her fandom research, her Tribexx twitter account, or the part about her wanting his secret book. He wiped a chocolate smudge from the corner of his mouth, shoved the frosting smeared napkin into the bag and then pulled out another donut and another napkin. "Any questions for me?"

So many. Too many. She shook her head, but stopped to say, "Hume told me to talk to you."

"Does she know about...about your visit to the basement?"

Although the counter was busy, they were the only ones in the seating area, so she kept her voice very soft. "I don't know. She told me to talk to you during that so-called meeting at The Southie. Before, before...the basement."

He leaned sideways to make room for a man carrying a crying toddler under one arm and pushing a bright red stroller containing a whining toy poodle with the other. After the man reached the exit, Guy continued. "She prefers to keep people in the dark. Makes them easier to manipulate, easier to get what she wants from them."

Hoping to get control of her nerves, Nidhi shoved her hands under her legs. "Sounds like an understatement."

"What was the meeting about?" he asked, assessing the new donut.

The man was outside now, kneeling beside the stroller, holding the little dog, and trying to comfort the crying kid by patting his tiny shoulder. Nidhi looked back to Guy. "Abandoned buildings."

"*Possessed* buildings," he countered.

She grinned at his sarcasm. "What the fuck ever."

They laughed.

She continued. "It sounds like she wants to get the kids in town to break into them, look for zombies. Maybe they make messes, cause trouble, then *they*—I don't know who yet—blame it on the Tribexxers. Could be a way to intimidate the Exxers. Get rid of them."

He lowered the donut he was about to bite into. "She told you all that?"

"No. She didn't tell me shit. I pieced that together."

"Not a bad take." He waved the donut at her. "Not bad at all because that sounds like something she'd cook up."

The man outside was walking off, the kid in his arms, snuggled into his shoulder. Again, she pulled her gaze back to Guy. "There's something in there about targeting certain buildings, but I haven't figured that out yet."

Guy bit into his donut, immediately getting chocolate frosting on his sunken cheek.

"I started at the paper in the summer, as an intern. She created a part time position for me." Back then that had seemed like a good thing, something the older woman had done to help out the next generation of women. "But I've been getting to know her more." And so now, everything was all different.

"What do you think she wants me for?" He broke a piece off the donut, studied it, then dropped it into his mouth.

The answer to that was just now coming to her. "Use you. Partly for click bait. Partly to give some validity to the theory about the possessions being connected to the tribe." She pulled her hands out from under her legs. "So," drew her thoughts together. "She wants to make fun of you again, but yeah, use you again, too."

"All those years of research and this is what I'm good for." He lifted his cup, swirling it as he raised the remains of the donut. "They respected me, back in the day. My work was ground-breaking. Original. Too original, it seems." He took a bite, added another smear of frosting to his face.

"I know about that book, your book. You know, the one Hayden wrote about in the article. I mean, articles."

"Haven't read it?" He took a sip then gazed out the window.

Now the sidewalk featured a stream of people crisscrossing over the bright blue background. "Can't get hold of a copy," she said.

He lowered the coffee cup and started tapping the bottom edge on the table.

"I would read it," she said, watching his blue eyes. "Not just the sex parts. The whole thing. If I had a copy."

He glanced up. "So you say."

"I really would." Honesty, for a change. It felt good. "It's related to my research."

He gave her his full attention. "Do tell."

And, while he sipped his coffee, she did tell.

All of it—the fandom-cult theory, the Tribexx twitter account, Mattie telling her about the secret book and her looking for it. Absolutely everything. Well, everything except the arrival of the mystery box that had shown up on her doorstep. Once she'd completed telling him everything but that, she asked, "What do you know about the abandoned, oh, excuse me, possessed, buildings?"

He down the last of his coffee and then rolled the empty cup between his hands. "Have you seen Hayden's list?"

She shrugged. "He and Mattie are making a map, I guess."

"I bet they are." He stopped rolling the cup. "Want my advice?"

"Does it include how to get rid of Mattie?"

He stuffed the cup into the bag then started crumpling the bag. "When it comes to her, the first thing you need to know is that she could appear at any time. Be ready."

"That won't help me get rid of her."

"For that, figure out what she wants and get it for her."

"I haven't a clue what she wants." Other than fucking her, and her life, up.

"Ask Hayden. He knows what she wants." With his hand still on the bag, Guy leaned forward. "What do you want, Nidhi?"

She put her hand on his bag, then leaned forward. "What do you want, Guy?"

"Touché'," he said, nodding slowly.

"Maybe we're going to be friends, Guy Belmont."

Still nodding, he said, "Maybe we are, Nidhi Bansal." He used the edge of the table to push himself to his feet. "Come with me. I want to show you something. And I have something someone gifted to me, but as it appears you have met the requirements and that it is more valuable to you than me, I would like to give it to you."

* * *

The sun was still out, making the sky an impossible cotton candy blue. Acorn Street was dotted with tourists. As often happened, when she passed them on her way to her front door, they looked away and pretended they just happened to be on the street. Then, once they were behind her, she could hear the click of the selfies. That afternoon, Nidhi was too amped up from her time with Guy to care.

She slipped inside without bothering to give the wanderers a knowing glance. Inside her townhouse, she dropped her bag on the hall table, then locked the door and engaged the deadbolt. Still standing by the door, she peeled off her sweater, itchy and stinking from nervous sweat, then kicked off her boots. Next, she stepped out of her jeans, dirty from being on the floor of the cage, then, knowing she'd never wear them again, added her bra and thong to the pile. She left the heap on her polished wood floor but took the bag containing the item she'd gotten in her trade with Guy to the kitchen. There, she set the crinkled, white grocery bag next to the only secret she'd kept from her new ally—the mysterious collection of evil, zombie shit.

Upstairs, she found her over-priced black robe, now tainted from the memory of the dream that turned out not to be a dream, slipped it on as she listened to a slew of voicemails from Easton. The first message, left about 24 hours ago, was about their plan for that night. The next few were increasingly annoyed, the final one a bit desperate. The silk billowed out behind her as she descended the stairs, pausing on the middle landing to hit his number.

His hello came after the third ring.

"I know, I know. I should've called sooner." She dove into several apologies, explaining that the work thing went a lot longer than she expected and that she'd been really distracted all day. In the kitchen, she put on the kettle, opened the plastic bag, then cut into the brown padded envelope tucked inside.

"Fine. Whatever." She could tell from his tone that he was done being annoyed and worried. "What time do you want me over there to get you?"

The only thing inside the envelope was a plus one invite to the Tribexx event she'd already planned on attending. The difference, this plastic, tag style invite was an all-access pass, getting her into the VIP lounge which was sure to be both disgusting and informative. "Um, I don't—"

"You want to meet there?" he asked.

One side of the tag was pink, the other white. This double-sided pass changed everything. "No, thanks though. I just… I just don't think I want to go." At the bottom of the grocery bag was a note. *Belmont plus 1.* Behind her, the kettle started to whistle, and she used the noise as an excuse to stop talking and think.

"What the hell?" Easton said once the whistle lowered to a hiss. "You've been waiting two weeks for this event."

She had been waiting that length of time. And she did need the interviews and photos. Just not with Easton. No way she could include him in this fucked up mess.

"The work thing was really intense. Not at all what I expected." That was honest. "I'm wiped out. I'll just wait for the next one."

"What about your research?"

She picked up the brown package the tag had been inside, flipped it over, looking for any markings she'd missed. "It's coming along fine, and I can always stalk them on social media." There was nothing written on the outside.

"True. Easy enough. They are pretty addicted to posting their stupid shit."

So true and in ways he'd never know about. Ways she never, ever wanted him, or anyone else she was close with, to know about.

"Are you sure about this?" His tone was softer. "We could take an Uber instead of the T, just go for a bit."

"I'm sure." She mashed the padded envelope into her overflowing paper recycling bin. "If I went, I'd have to come up with something to wear, you know, and... I'm just not feeling it tonight." She put the plastic bag in its own overflowing bin.

He mumbled his acceptance then started telling her about his day with Sayo, his girlfriend. She put him on speaker, poured hot water into her mug, dropped in a tea bag, and continued to half listen while she texted Hayden. Easton was still talking while she dug through her closet to find her black thigh high boots and tightest jeans. Add in a black T-shirt and she'd be good enough. About the time she was tightening the laces on her boots, Hayden's reply, agreeing to meet her at the T stop, pinged in her messages. Still listening to Easton and adding in a comment or two of her own, she went to her bathroom and started on her hair and make-up. Soon, she was begging off, telling her bestie she had to climb into bed, while she was climbing down the stairs. She stopped in the kitchen, stuck a knife into her jacket pocket and poked a whole in the lining. She set the knife down, grabbed one of the vials from the collection and slipped it in through the hole. Then she stuffed in wallet in and pushed them both deep into the lining. After they said she and Easton said their goodbyes and clicked off, she unlatched the deadbolt and stepped outside. Then, thinking about her return, she did something she only did when her parents nagged her—she set the alarm.

Chapter Ten

"You're already sad that no one will give a shit about
your fucked up MeToo story?"

She took the T to the Green Street stop in Jamaica Plain,
where she waited for Hayden beside a trash can
overflowing with fast food bags. The clouds, high and
streaking across the sky, let some of the final rays of the
early spring sun through, making the late afternoon one of
those perfect spring days everyone raves about. She knew
from her parents that gentrification was an issue in that
particular community, so she wasn't surprised to see
construction trucks parked on curbs. The sidewalk was a
mix of fast-walking fitness singles, harried-looking college
students, and teenagers, phone in hand, head down low. An
occasional dog walker passed, each of them wearing ear
buds or full-size headphones. After about 20 minutes,
Hayden hopped out of the train car, wearing the same
canvas work jacket and brown boots as the night before.

All she offered was a single word greeting. "Hey."

He didn't reply, instead tipped his head indicating
for her to follow. She did. Once away from the station,
they dodged a pizza driver coming around the corner
without slowing. They kept walking, cutting through
Johnson Park. They reached the end of the park, then
crossed the street.

Once they were on the sidewalk again, he looked over. "Are you sure you want to do this?"

They continued walking, side by side, occasionally one of them dodged a person, pet, or both. "Yeah, I'm sure." She stuffed her hands into the pocket of her black bomber jacket, felt the glass vile hidden in the lining, then wrapped her fingers around the plastic tag. "I need to ask you a question. How do I get rid of her?"

He replied without looking over. "You don't."

"You did."

His mouth pulled down. "Things between me and her aren't what they seem. The only thing you can be certain of is that none of this is what it seems."

She thought about Belmont, what he'd shown her in the basement of *The Globe* office building, the collection of vials Elizabeth apparently referred to as her doomsday prep kit. The liquids were on standby, *in case we need to nullify them*, were her words. Or at least what Guy said were her words. "No shit," she said, confirming that things were not at all what they seemed. Her chest tightened; she exhaled, willing herself to continue. "I what… wait until she's bored with me, done with… whatever?"

He nodded. "Yeah. That's about it. Unless you can help her get what she really wants."

She waited.

"She wants the same thing we all want. A way out."

She couldn't be hearing him right. "A way out of the tribe?"

"Yep."

"In the meantime, she won't—"

"Hurt you? Not physically. Not in an extreme way, at least. She won't do the ritual on you either. Unless you ask for it. For them, it's a choice."

"A choice to be left on a shelf, wrapped in burlap, for who the hell knows how long."

"Yeah."

But not the sex. After what she'd been through just in the past 48 hours, she'd bet some of their victims begged for the ritual just to get away from the abuse. No doubt Hayden had been through some horrific shit. She watched his jaw, clenching and unclenching, his eyes darting up and down the street. "How much farther?" she asked, looking from one structure to the next. The street was an appealing blend of old and new, cozy and modern.

"Not far." He pointed to a weathered brick building at the end of the street.

The very end of the block was a piece of vacant land that had been converted into a dog park. The one he pointed to was the last in the row of painted wood buildings, long and narrow with what appeared to be two fronts, one on each street. "Which side of the building has the entrance?"

"VIP on this side. Everyone else, the other side."

Of course. Can't have the VIPs going in on the same side of the street as the rest.

"What's on the other side?" she asked.

"Tea shop bakery thing," he replied.

They continued walking, silently, side by side, until he pulled to a stop about ten feet from the door of a boutique bookstore called The Archive. She leaned against the brick wall. An Uber pulled up to the curb, let out two college age girls, both in full gear. One had a coil of rope circling her shoulder, the other carried a riding crop. The one with the rope held a plastic event tag like the one Nidhi had tucked in her jacket. After the pair slipped through the door to the bookstore, Nidhi pulled her tag out. The characteristic X took up most of the print space. Down at the bottom, handwritten in a Sharpie, was the date and a set of initials she couldn't make out. Only someone familiar with the emerging Tribexx culture would know how to interpret the card.

"Where'd you get that, by the way?"

"Someone left it on my front step."

He lifted an eyebrow.

She shrugged then tucked the card back into her pocket.

"Are you certain about doing this?" he asked.

"I need to go in there. I don't have a choice."

"There's always a choice." He started walking again. speaking over his shoulder. "But sometimes both choices suck."

She shoved off the wall and fell into step beside him.

He reached for the door. She stopped him from opening it by putting her hand on his arm. "Thanks for trying, you know, to warn me."

He acknowledged her words with a slight pull on his mouth. She followed him in, bells chiming overhead as they moved into the room.

The small shop had a dark academia vibe, with a mix of wooden shelves and tables overloaded with books and accented with intriguing collectibles. A pair of over-stuffed leather chairs filled a far corner, a small, faux candle lit chandelier hanging above them. The display at the front of the store featured a collection of philosophy. Nidhi recognized the cover of *Beyond Good and Evil* and *Apology of Socrates*. The other thing she noticed, as they passed through the shop, was the thick scent swelling into the room. Dank weed and some type of cleaning fluid. Hayden pointed to a handwritten sign taped to the wall beside the start of the narrow hallway. A white sheet of printer paper with two symbols: X, and below that, an arrow.

They walked in the direction indicated by the arrow, him in front and her behind. Pictures and plaques hung on the wall near a pair of restrooms, and she scanned them as they moved. The photos appeared to be authors who'd come to the shop to sign books. Those weren't especially noteworthy. It was the small one hanging across from the manager's office that made her grab Hayden's jacket and pull him to a stop.

He turned around.

She ran her finger across the top of the gold gilt frame.

The certificate was an award of excellence given to Historics by Hume, the design studio that had apparently done the renovations and interior design.

The grantor was Bansal Properties.

Nidhi stared at the words, trying to decipher the meaning, the implications of her parents being connected to Elizabeth Hume's husband. Something? Nothing? Everything?

Hayden tugged on her sleeve. She took one last look then left it behind.

The thump of cyberpunk techno, like the industrial music at The Southie, increased in volume as the hallway twisted and turned. As they went, the lights above grew dimmer, the smell thickened, with the addition of sweat, beer, and something that made Nidhi's stomach clench. There was a fuchsia door on the left side near the end of the hall. Across from it, a woman perched on a tall stool. Beside her was a tall table, piled with lanyards and a brown wood box. A giant wad of pink gum was visible between her teeth as her deep red lips opened and closed in rhythm to the music coming from within.

Nidhi slipped the card from her jacket, lifted it, and flipped it to show both sides.

The woman gave Hayden a critical once over, the motion of her mouth stopping for a few seconds. "You the plus one?" she nearly barked to be heard over the music.

He barked back. "Yep."

She hopped off the stool and blocked the entrance. "I don't know you." Mouth closed, briefly, she gazed into Nidhi's face. Mouth opened again, talking around the wad of gum, she said, "I don't know either of you."

Hayden raised his hand and stuck the gaudy gold pinky ring he always wore in the woman's face.

She blinked hard. "Oh fuck." She reached over, grabbed two lanyards and another plastic tag style VIP pass from inside the box. "Clip the shit together and keep the card in view. Pink side up if you're viewing. White side up if you're into participating. I don't need to tell you what it means if you take it off."

After Hayden accepted the items, she cleared out of the way, hopped back on to the stool and yelled, "Have a great night, you lucky luckies."

Hayden pulled the door open, then handed Nidhi the lanyard. After clipping the card to it, she looped the thing over her head. Hayden did the same, then pointed to her plastic tag as he leaned in to yell over the rumble from the room beyond the threshold. "Don't take it off. And be sure to keep the pink side up."

Side by side, they went through the door, stepped into another hallway. This one shorter, only about 5 feet long and empty. The music was very loud now, the mixture of smells intense. Without slowing, Hayden yanked the final door open. He swooped his arm behind her and ushered her in.

They'd come into the venue from the back. In front of them was a mob wearing black leather, tattered white T-shirts, and red tube tops. There were lots of torn fishnets, boots, shaved heads, and tribe inspired, shaded tattoos as well. All the bodies swayed, vibing to the music. No phones in sight, everyone was connected in real time, grabbing each other, laughing, playing with ropes and chains, making out. Obviously, the Tribexxers were fans of this fucked up culture. They wanted to dress like the tribe, to act like the tribe. Be like the tribe. Thought doing so was fun, a meaningful method of self-expression. If only they understood how fucking stupid they were. How degrading and dangerous the whole scene was.

Nidhi stayed behind Hayden, fine with letting him shove through the crowd, creating a path for them. Heat of bodies and the pressure of their flesh assaulted her, but she pushed her way through, keeping Hayden's tan canvas coat in view. He stopped at a railing, and she worked her way up to get beside him. They stood at the edge of an observation deck. Below was another, less subdued, mass of bodies. That group was much bigger, denser, and more aggressive. Apparently, the VIP crowd was too elite to slam. That group also had some mostly naked couples, off to the side, bodies jerking, pulsing, arms snaking as they created their own live sex show. Apparently, the VIP group was also too elite to fuck.

To the left were stairs that descended to the pit. The room below had black walls and a black floor. The space was filled with gyrating bodies, a blur of motion. At the top of the stairs, and also at the bottom, stood a single man wearing a heavy black cloak. Nidhi scanned the smaller crowd surrounding them. Everyone, dancing, kissing, preening, they all had the same plastic VIP tag she and Hayden wore, pink side up. Nidhi checked hers.

Hayden clutched the railing, that golden ring catching the lights from above. She'd always assumed it was a fraternity ring or a family crest, some symbol of the past, a flashy reminder of something that once mattered in his life. Now she understood, he was either an enemy or an ally. Somehow, he was one of them.

She tapped the gold ring with her finger, lifted her eyebrows.

He leaned over, shouted in her ear. "If things go bad, I can't help you."

"Can't or won't?" she shouted back.

He lifted his hand, jabbed the underside of the ring with his thumb. "Can't."

He set his hand back down and turned his gaze to the rowdy crowd below, staring into the river of writhing bodies, shifting to the pulsing techno. Nidhi joined him, watching the crowd sway, bounce, and fuck. An electric current ran through the air, buzzing above the mob, uniting them, creating a hungry tension. Nidhi focused on a girl wearing a black leather mini-dress leaning into the guard positioned at the bottom of the stairs. She tucked her arms under the cloak, moved closer, pressing herself tightly against his naked body. When she tried to kiss his chest, he swept his arm up between them then to the side, brushing her off and sending her stumbling backwards.

She leaned into Hayden, yelled, "What's this about?"

"Whatever it is, it'll be fucking awful."

She continued staring at him.

"They never announce the main event in advance. People just show up and wait."

And wait she did. Her legs cramped. Sweat rolled down her back. She wished she could text Easton. She waited some more. Her patience turned into frustration, but still she studied the partiers. Below, the crowd continued thriving, dancing, getting thicker. The music continued to beat, thumping through the room, making the people move. The couples along the wall, still fucking, obviously got off on being on display. There were a few naked bodies chained to the wall. Men, women, she couldn't tell. Behind her, the VIPs had settled, most of them still clustered together as they too watched the crowd below.

After what felt like an hour, the loud chime of a church bell cut through the music. The techno continued but at a lower volume, and now including an indecipherable voice track, a series of hurried whispers. The bell chimed again. The music went lower. Strobe lights appeared from above, dropping down from the ceiling as the beams offered an off-putting mixture of green and yellow. In the far-right corner, a circle opened, the crowd moved back, compacting toward the opposite side. Some people stumbled while others shrunk back, curling into themselves and scurrying to get out of the way. Still others moved slowly, apparently reluctant to make way or unwilling to merge with the mass of faceless bodies getting pushed back and away from the lighted center of the pit.

Chapter Eleven
"Whatever it is, it'll be fucking awful."

Gradually the reason for the disruption came into view. It was an empty wooden cage, like the one she'd been confined to but smaller, being carried into the center of the pit. Poles stuck out from the corner of each end. Each of the poles rested on the shoulders of a cloaked man. From behind the first cage, came another of the exact same size. Then another, also carried by cloaked bearers. The bearers, all naked beneath long fur cloaks, set the cages in a row, side by side. There were five in all, all the same size and each empty.

Once all five were down, a woman wearing nothing except a pair of white leather shorts strutted out from the same doorway in the back right corner. As she walked, she raised her arms, encouraging the crowd to howl and cheer. When she stopped beside the first cage, the roar of the crowd stopped. It was then that Nidhi spotted the pair of nipple clamps pinching her swaying tits. The clamps were connected by a rhinestone chain that caught the reflection of the strobes above, tiny bright dots of light flickered around the pit.

The woman lifted the narrow end of the cage, got down on her hands and knees and scrambled inside. Once in, she circled like a cat, using the motion of her arms and

132

legs to make her ass sway. She paused, arching her back and shaking her shoulders, her face turned upward as she howled. Once all the air was out of her lungs, she crept back out of the cage and sat cross-legged just outside the opening. She took hold of the rhinestone chain connecting her tits and lifted. It was then that Nidhi noticed the neon glitter covering the woman's entire body. While the woman continued shaking the chain, making her breasts jiggle and bounce, she rolled her shoulders, her skin rippled and sparkled beneath the lights. The crowd raised their arms and cheered. After several long seconds, she released the chain and settled into her seated position, staring straight ahead. The crowd quieted to a hush. The techno music thrummed with an expectant rhythm.

Again, the crowd began to vibrate. Near the front, people pointed, others grabbed one and other and shoved them forward. One man, wearing only a black leather kilt, circled the cage, his arms jerking above his head as he skipped in a zip zagged circle. Once the man merged with the crowd, one of the cloaked men who carried the cage into the room raised his arm. A hush fell.

Another woman came out, this one wore a black lace corset and thigh high boots. The corset started above her shaved pussy. The laces had been pulled tight, forcing her breasts to spill out of the top. She stopped at the second cage, turned her back to the crowd then squatted and grabbed the sides of the cage. Still holding on to the wooden slats, she straightened her legs, showing off the deep groove between her thighs. One of the cloaked bearers strutted forward, his arm outstretched, his fingers wide. He swept his hand downward in a steep angle, his palm smacking one side of her ass. She flinched but did not let go of the cage. In rhythm to the music, he rose and lowered his arm, delivering body shaking smacks. After five strikes, he moved to the other side, giving the audience a view of her reddened ass cheek. Five swats for the other side. When he finished, both of her ass cheeks were pink, her shoulders were slumped. He gave her one last smack on her thigh before strutting away. She let go of the cage, dropped to her hands and knees and went into the cage. Inside she paused, and with her back to the crowd, rose up on her knees. She reached back to caress her abused ass, using slow circles to smooth the battered skin. The crowd applauded and cheered, encouraging her. She took hold of her ass, arched her back and spread the cheeks apart. Another round of applause. She dropped to her hands and knees then slunk backward to get out. Beside the opening of the cage, she crumpled to the ground then lay curled into a tight ball.

Again, the crowd rolled with tremors of excitement. One woman stepped forward, lifted her skirt to reveal her own bare ass, then spanked herself. The crowd cheered until the man silenced them with a raise of his hand.

Next out was a man, being led by a leash. The cloaked leader took a few steps, tugged sharply on the leash, then waited for the man on the ground to follow. The chained man's face was covered by a black leather mask with only a hole for his mouth. Once the bearer had his position in front of the cage, he dropped the leash, pulled a flask from his side, removed a stopper, and then poured some oil into the palm of his hand.

Hayden leaned close and spoke directly into her ear. "It's probably ritual oil, very potent." He moved back, watching the two men below before pulling his gaze away and adding, "Very dangerous."

The leader rubbed the oil across the man's chest,

using a circular motion that started by his collar bone and worked his way lower over his abdomen. After skipping his cock, he moved to his thighs. He lifted his hand then pushed him to turn him around. He poured more into his palm and coated the man's back and ass. Once done, he shoved the man to the ground. The man got to his hands and knees, then crawled into the cage. He spun around on his knees a couple times and then came back out. Once beside the door, he sat on the ground in front of the cage, his ass on his heels, his cock growing hard and erect.

Nidhi waited for the festive reaction of the crowd, but this time there was none. The people below remained as still as they had when the leashed man first stepped into the cleared circle of the pit. The tension of the crowd rose upward, like a vapor, and she breathed it in. The relaxed ease that had been in the small area around her was gone and in its place was an evil energy, an uncertain dread that promised harm.

The bass in the music grew heavier and the rhythm of the music slowed. Another church bell sounded, this time lower, deeper, making the air reverberate. The man in the center of the pit stepped toward the crowd in front of him. They all remained frozen, their arms and legs totally motionless as he searched through them. After a long moment, he backed up, turned his gaze above, to the gallery. The tension surrounding her intensified, so electric it made her palms burn and her throat went dry.

The man raised his arm and pointed.

Behind her a series of hushed murmurs began, she turned back to find most of the other people backing away from the railing, leaving only her, Hayden, and a few others. Many in the crowd were gripping their plastic tags, holding them slightly raised, pink side out. Hayden too was holding his aloft, pink side out. He was staring at her, his wide-eyed gaze a mixture of horror and distress. She reached down for her tag, ready to raise it, pink side out, but it was gone. She dug into her jacket. Nothing. She opened her jacket, flipped the sides back, but the tag was gone. The lanyard hung loose, the clip still there, but the tag—gone.

Below the man in the pit was still pointing, the end of his finger aimed directly at her. She bent down, scanned the floor. The rest of the people were now backing away, isolating her and Hayden alone at the rail. She dropped to her knees, scrambling side to side, but there was nothing on the grimy carpet beneath her hands. And then she spotted it, down below, on the floor of the pit. It lay there, white side up.

Nidhi pushed against Hayden. He grabbed her arm, squeezing tightly, trying to stop her, but she yanked free and rushed to the steps. The bouncer at the top moved aside. Hayden was calling to her but all she could think about was getting the tag. Taking the stairs two at a time, she rushed down, only to be stopped by the bouncer at the bottom. He grabbed the collar of her jacket, she shrugged out of his grip, then tried again to go get the tag.

He blocked her way, pointing to the center of the pit. "Disciples must obey. Go now. The ceremony master is calling for you."

She was close enough now that she could see the master's slender face beneath his hood. The strobe lights above continued to cut through the center of the pit, slicing through the blackness, cutting the images into pieces. The crowd's bodies remained motionless. Their eyes all remained focused on her. None of them made an effort to help her even though it must have been obvious what she needed to do—get the tag, prove her right to be there, and hold up the pink side. The master's mouth twisted into what could be a snarl or a leer as he marched forward, flinging the long cloak out of his way as he came toward them. She tried again to dodge left, the guard grabbed her arm, and pulled. She fought, yanking her arm then leaning back, trying to use her weight to break free. She was no match for him, he easily jerked her off her feet, then lifted her again until she barely had her feet beneath her. He continued squeezing her arm as he dragged her forward only releasing her once the master held her other arm.

She twisted, searching her surroundings, but the roaming lights above her made it impossible to tell which direction she faced. Hayden had to be there, somewhere. She pulled against the new grip, trying to see which direction the stairs were in so that she could run to the tag. Once she had it in her hands, this would all stop.

"I didn't take it off on purpose," she yelled at him.

His voice was even louder. "Disciples must be respectful." The man dragged her toward the third cage. She yelled again.

The music had begun to pulse, growing louder so that no amount of yelling or screaming would make a difference. The metallic rhythm made the air shake, made her skin vibrate. Or was that fear.

Terror.

The fresh wave of anguish tore through her. She twisted, pulling back then grabbing her own arm and trying to pull it loose. When that didn't work, she pried his fingers, clawing him with her nails, then leaned back, again trying to use her body weight to get free. Finally, she opened her mouth wide, bent low, aiming for the soft spot on the inside of his wrist. Just as she was an inch away from making contact, she went up in the air, an arm was wrapped around her waist. Another person grabbed her free arm. She was being carried toward the now open fourth cage.

A scream tore out from deep in her chest. She threw her head back and howled, but still they lowered her down until she was level with the cage. And then they threw her in.

As soon as she was inside, the cage was turned upright, forcing her to the bottom while one of the bearers slid the door into place from above. She grabbed at the lock, but a hand came from nowhere and took hold of her wrist. The lock was clicked into place and the cage was lowered to the ground.

One of the guards bent down beside her and waved her over. She put her head close to the wooden slats. "Thank you for contributing to the show. You are a good performer. Keep it up and you will be rewarded."

A spotlight came on, shining on the master, who once again stood in the center of the room. He'd begun the ritual again, scanning the lower crowd before moving up to the VIP deck. He walked from one end of the pit to the other, then stopped. He turned his back to the crowd and held an outstretched arm to the cloaked men in the back. One of the men jogged forward, the edges of his cloak fluttering behind him, exposing his bare ass. After he pulled to a stop, he knelt down, swept his arm across himself and then offered up the flask of oil. The master took the oil, spun on his heels, returned to the center of the pit. He held the flask a loft.

The spotlight moved beyond him, the light gradually progressing from one face to another. Each person held a pink tag or tapped the one dangling on their chest.

Nidhi saw Hayden, his face blank, the pink tag still laying midway down his canvas coat.

I can't help you.

That couldn't be true. She stared at him, willed him to look back, to see her, but it was too dark, too loud, and she was apparently too far gone. The spotlight slid over to the woman beside him. She lifted the tag pinched between her fingers. The spotlight shifted. The music continued booming and grinding. The spotlight stopped on a man in black jeans, a black cape with a hood pulled down low. No tag. No lanyard. Only a collection of silver chains shining in the spotlight.

Nidhi tugged on the lock hanging from the cage door. It was secure. She shook each bar, one by one.

The crowd surrounding the pit shifted. The two sides were splitting apart, creating a river of empty space between them. The man came down the stairs then stood in the gap. He threw the sides of the cape over his shoulders, revealing a wide, lean body. The fabric of the cape bunched up on his back, flapping as he walked forward. The master held the flask up and offered it to the man when he reached the edge of the pit. The man dropped to his hands and knees, one side of the cape fell, and he dragged it along as he crawled forward, going directly into the cage.

The master closed the door, put the lock into place.

The crowd roared. Arms in the air, jerking, swaying, slithering, the crowd surged forward. The entire mass of people continued forward, rushing to surround the cages like waves crashing on the shore. A sea of legs surrounded her. The other cages disappeared. The cage started to shake. People took hold of the bars. Hands came in, grabbing her clothes, grabbing her hands, her legs, her hair. She jerked and pulled away, freeing herself only to be caught again. New hands took hold of the slats, shook the cage. All the howling and screaming carried over the music pulsing and shuddering through the air. Nidhi rolled into a ball, but that did nothing to break her away from the rush of horror. She reached over her head, swept her hair down, held it to her neck. Occasionally a slice of the light cut through the bodies, caught her in the eyes.

She squeezed her eyes shut.

The race of her heart, the clenching of her chest, if she didn't get a grip on herself, she'd pass out. What then? Staying in the tight ball, she concentrated on her breath. She blocked out the sounds, the smells. Thought about her breath. Gradually, the urgency of the hands eased. She opened her eyes. Much of the crowd was now focusing on the other cages. Two men and three women still surrounded her, taunting her with mock tears. The captive in the cage beside her, the man in the mask, was wiping oil from himself and offering it to those outside. One after the other, people tried to get some of the oil, swiping it onto their necks or chests as soon as they had it on their hand.

The man on her right, the one with the hood, had unzipped his pants and was massaging his cock. The crowd around him was laughing and chanting, urging him on. The women captives were also soaking up the adoration of the crowd, letting those outside the cage touch them, grab their legs, their arms, to do whatever they could by reaching through the slats.

Just a show, she told herself.

This whole disgusting display was just a show.

Part of the Tribexx fandom she' been so anxious to see, to be part of. No wonder Belmont had written some of his experiences under a different name. None of this experience could ever be included in her research either. In the end though, using the pseudonym did him no good; he'd still gotten shunned from academia. The same thing wasn't going to happen to her.

She sat up, straightened her legs, and let go of her hair. She forced her shoulders back and scanned the gallery. Hayden must still be there. No matter how he felt about her, how rude she'd been to him, he wouldn't have left her. Would he? He needed something from the night, too. Otherwise, he wouldn't have come.

The lights above changed colors, turning to all green. The music also changed, from the heavy industrial techno to something similar but smoother. The sounds were still deep, with an edge to them, but now gave the atmosphere a new entrancing, captivating vibe. Hungry. Sexual.

The perfect backdrop for the captives on display.

On cue, the crowd fell back, flattening themselves to the far wall. A stream of guards came rushing from the back, each carrying chairs. They set up a row, then returned with more chairs. Set up another. Soon the rows filled the space, and the guests filled the seats. Some swayed to the beat, some bounced up and down. Once the crowd was seated, another crew wearing all black appeared. A screen was being lowered from above, the giant thing wobbling as it came down, slicing the place in half.

* * *

Hayden worked his way through the gallery crowd. The voyeurs on the landing were less forgiving now that the threat of being selected was past and the next phase of the show would begin soon. The mass pressed forward, waiting for the moment when they'd be granted open access to stairs so they all could descend and get a seat below.

He should've known the event was an auction. He should've warned Nidhi what could happen if she wasn't careful. He grabbed the shoulder of a bald guy who'd planted himself near the top of the steps and tugged the guy backward.

"Suck me, asshole," the guy muttered, coming back at him.

Hayden whistled and held up his hand. The guard spotted the gold band and whistled in reply. Then reached into the crowd with both arms and shoved people out of the way. Hayden passed through the crowd, feeling the press of the bodies as people filled in behind him as he moved toward the stairs. He jogged down, showed the ring to the guard at the bottom. Five pairs of guards came out from the back, heading toward the cages. The crowd continued streaming over to the chairs. Those already seated stared at the blank screens, the fabric still quivering. By the time he arrived at the clearing, the guards were squatting beneath the poles sticking out from the corners of the cages. The master lifted one arm. Each bearer raised one arm. The master lifted his other arm. All the bearers dropped their arm and then stood, lifting all five cages in unison.

The master dropped his arms.

The guards moved, lock-stepping, taking the cages away from the rows of chairs and disappearing behind the screen. Five more screens were being set up around the pit. The VIP crowd had been released from above and were rushing to stand in front of the smaller screens set up along the sides of the room. Soon there were clusters of attendees gathered around each one. Hayden weaved through the VIP crowd, made his way to the last cage in the row. Far off at the end of the room, the first cage disappeared into a tunnel. The second followed. The woman's face was pressed between the bars.

A smile or grimace?

The cage vanished into the darkness of the tunnel.

He continued walking, circling the edges of the rows of chairs and then cutting behind the screen. The third cage was next, disappearing into the tunnel. Nidhi was seated with her back to him, crossed-legged with her arms outstretched, her hands gripping the bars, holding herself steady. Then she was gone.

The fifth cage went next.

Then, they were all gone.

He lingered in the empty space between the crowd and the tunnel.

A man stood and pointed at him, raising his arm, a pointed finger at the end of it. The guy's mouth opened, turning into a wide black circle. The woman beside him turned and stared. She too opened her mouth, began to yell. And then a third.

Hayden lifted his hands, tapping the pinky ring on one hand with the forefinger of the other. Their mouths snapped shut and they spun back toward the vacant screen. A lone body was moving toward him, coming slowly past the rows. Even though he couldn't see his face he knew that awkward shuffling gait.

* * *

Nidhi's eyes adjusted to the dim light in the tunnel. The smell of cold dirt swirled around her, growing more intense as they moved deeper into the underground. The cage bounced. The rhythm of the stepping was even, but she could tell they were descending slightly. Any hope that confinement was just part of an act was gone, and so the waves of panic had become constant. She held onto the bars, squeezing the wood so tightly her fingers had become numb, her wrists ached.

The music from the event had faded into silence. A throaty hum gradually coming from the opposite direction replaced it. The light in front of Nidhi continued to grow brighter. The sound grew louder. The sound was worse than the cage it was coming from. The cage, she understood. The sound, she did not. Its unnatural whine, desperate and lonely yet also threatening. The carrier followed the others into another open area. Mellow lighting skimmed across the moist fieldstone walls surrounding the space. The wide center area was dim. Cables and electrical cords hung like black vines creeping down the walls and crawling across the floor. There were six stations, each had a monitor and web cam near the wall, a large number 1-7, painted on the cement floor in front of the screen. Spot 6 was already occupied.

Inside that cage was a naked woman, or what was at one time a human woman. Shoulder length hair, matted and snarled, stuck out at odd angles around her head. Her small body was compact and muscular. Her face, contorted, grey lips pulled back, teeth snapping as she exhaled the guttural growl. Squatting on her muscular haunches, arms tucked between her thighs, she looked like she would thrust forward and attack. But of course, she couldn't.

144

Not yet.

She, *it*, continued gnashing its teeth, whining, and watching.

The first cage, the one holding the woman with the set of glittering nipple clamps, was placed on number 1. One of the bearers took a wood block from a stack near the wall and placed it on top of the cage. A large, bold pink 1 painted on the block for number 1. She reached up, touched the underside of the wood with her fingertips. Number 2 was next. After the painted wood block featuring the 2 was placed on top, the bearers left. While number 3 was being positioned, the fabric screens hanging in front of the cages blinked brightly, revealing what each one of the five web cams captured—the individual captives in the cages. The numbers on top. Number 4 for Nidhi.

The row of the screens was about ten feet from the wall. A cloaked woman sat in the back corner, a laptop across her knees, an empty chair on one side of her, another fabric screen hanging from the ceiling on the another. That screen displayed a twitter feed. The posts fed quickly, clicking up and refreshing in seconds.

#tribexx in all of them. #yesno an #noyes in most of them.

A new picture in picture image popped up on screens 1-5. Each of the additional images was sexual. The picture in picture video of the man captive beside her showed him sucking off another man. The two of them chained together, a third man watching. Nidhi's was from the night Mattie had gotten into her brownstone.

Mattie on top of her, Mattie touching her.

Nidhi's glazed eyes, roaming.

Mattie stroking Nidhi's clit.

Nidhi's mouth, opening, letting a groan break free.

The woman continued attacking the keyboard.

New hashtags appeared in the feed.

#1yesno

#2yesno

#3yesno

#4noyes

#5yesno

#6trueexx

The picture in picture images continued, looping each time the images concluded.

The woman in the thigh high boots turned her ass to the camera and smacked her ass cheeks. The woman wearing the nipple clamps held onto the top of the cage and shimmied.

The hashtags, now only with the #1 and a row of numbers after the yesno. The woman in the corner pounded the keyboard. The numbers went up, continued going up, until stopping suddenly. #2 next. Then #3. The person in the corner brushed back the hood and yelled. "4 has a stop order."

Two bearers stepped in.

"You heard me." She called, pointing to Nidhi. "Stop order."

"Who—"

"Doesn't matter who. I verified it."

The pair of bearers opened the door. "Get out."

Their hands fell to their sides.

One bent down. "Some dirty fuck out there likes you, wants to be your savior."

Nidhi crawled forward.

They both stepped back.

Nidhi scrambled out and backed away toward the hallway. Another bearer appeared, grabbed her elbow. At the end of the hallway, he stopped. "Watch your back. I bet they're waiting for you out there." He shoved her.

The crowd was still seated, viewing the live stream for #5. As in the other room, the screen was split, showing the captive in the cage now with another video beside it. Nidhi moved to the wall and braced herself. The additional video showed the man lying on a blanket in an empty warehouse. Mattie, naked, mounted on top of the man, riding him hard, grinding into him as she rocked. Each time she thrust; the man's head lulled side to side. His eyes were shut. He was unconscious.

Nidhi tapped the shoulder of the woman closest to her then leaned down to ask, "Are there two videos for each?" she asked, pointing to the screen in front of them.

"Yeah." She spun back around, looked Nidhi up and down. "That was you! Yours was awesome. Where did ya'll film that? It looked like a movie set. Perfect." The girl jabbed the guy beside her, started jabbing everyone nearby while tipping her head toward Nidhi. Soon, dozens of gazes were on her. Mouths opened and closed.

"Fucking hot."

"It looked so real."

"How did you get picked?"

Nidhi backed away, flattened herself to the wall. How many people in the VIP gallery? Each of them drugged and assaulted?

To get to the stairs, she stayed close to the wall, keeping her head tipped away from the crowd. The gallery space was vacant, the guard by the entrance door, gone. The stool she'd been perched on, also gone. The thumping faded completely by the time she reached the final door. She pushed through, paused at the plaque listing her parents' company, but not even the curiosity over that was enough to make her linger.

"I hear it didn't go as expected."

Guy, sitting on one of the overstuffed leather chairs, an open book on his lap. The lamp beside him casting a warm glow across his face, his phone and an empty teacup on the table between the two cozy chairs.

"I've heard of a stop order but never actually seen one happen. So, congratulations on that."

"Congratulations on not getting sold?"

"Technically, you did get sold. Someone paid for your release. It's the same process as buying a captive for the night the only difference..." He lifted one hand, palm up, gesturing toward her.

"The buyer doesn't get to torment you." Her hands were starting to shake, her facial muscles quivering. "Fuck you? Fuck with you? Fucking torture you?" Her stomach too, was tense and turning.

"That's right." He closed the book. "They simply let you go."

She wanted to ask what happened to the captives, afterward. After the buyers had had their fun. Yet, she didn't really want to know. Or she did, in fact, already know. "What're you doing here?"

"Did you get the information you needed?" he asked.

Oh, yes. The information. The evidence. She shrugged. "What good is it though? No one is going to believe that this," she motioned to the hallway, "is the recruiting process."

"It is effective though. Can't really not join them once you've been… inducted. Bit late then, eh? It's a get what you ask for and more situation, hm?"

He was right. Each of these captives appeared to have come to the event willingly and, with the exception

148

of her, enthusiasm and desire. Then again, was she being honest with herself? Hadn't she wanted to know everything. To experience everything? "But they didn't know…"

"We never know what we don't know. Until it is too late." He put the book on the table, picked up his phone and then braced his hands on his thighs to steady himself as he got to his feet.

He shuffled past. "Guy?" She called to him when his hand was wrapped around the doorknob.

He turned back.

"Why did you come here?"

"Have you forgotten? I have a horse in this race."

Her mind was filled only with the memory of her cage. The other cages. The thing in number 6.

"Our arrangement?" When she remained silent, he added, "The trade?"

It clicked. He hadn't come to make sure she was safe or to offer help if she got into trouble. He'd come to make sure she survived the night in some sort of state that would enable her to fulfill her end of the trade.

"Oh, right. Of course."

"You'll let me know about the meeting? Where and when?"

"I will."

He nodded. The bells on the door chimed, the sound continuing even after he disappeared onto the street. She picked up the teacup, raised it. Chamomile. She turned the book over. Nietzsche, the one from the display by the door. She returned it to the stack on the table. The bells chimed, and she was back out on the street.

Outside, the night air was crisp, humid, and breezy. No moon, no stars. Just the blue-black sky.

"Nidhi Bansal. The Nidhi, Nidhi girl. Not so needy tonight, are you?"

The man coming around from the side of the building wore a skintight, long-sleeve black T-shirt, military style jacket and a black leather kilt. His arms were twisted upward, his shoulders undulating behind his head as he whistled to her. The silver rings in his ears visible behind his long black hair. Grabbing his hair in one hand, he skipped over and stopped directly in front of her, held out the other hand.

"Touch me. I need your magic."

She put her palm in his. He took hold of her hand, raised his arm and spun them both around.

"Now we both have the magic." He let go and smacked his arms to his sides. "Rod McKinon? Hello? Don't you remember our epic bonfire?"

His absurd, mock hurt expression made her laugh. "Yes, now I do. You're," she looked around at the empty street, "out of context."

He pointed at the door she'd just come through. "We have this in common, didn't you know?"

The leather clothes, heavy boots, and the living on the edge personality it all made sense. She should have known he was a Tribexxer. "I do now," she said, taking a step back.

"Aren't you glad though? Aren't you happy to see a friendly face? I am the friendly face; in case you didn't guess." He wrapped his arm behind her back and leaned into her. "Where are you headed, friendly friend?"

"Home?" To relive that night in her mind? To sit on her bed and read the #Tribexx feed? No thanks.

"It's too early for that."

Call Easton? What could she possibly say? She hung

back, resisting his pull. "Were you inside? At the...
event?"

"No ticket. I tried to get one," he frowned. "You
didn't get one either?"

"I don't want to go in there," she said.

"Me either. I really did want to get in, but the
spectacle is probably over by now. So, there's no point."
He pulled harder, forcing her to either jerk away or go
along beside him. "Too early to go home. And I have
something to show you. Something you, Nidhi Bansal,
are going to really, really like."

She watched him from the corner of her eyes as she
gave in and let him pull her down the sidewalk. The wind
lifted his hair, and it hit her in the face. After she brushed
it away, she spotted a fleeting shadow in the distance.
They moved along, Rod beside her, talking about the
party where the two of them had made the giant bon fire,
finishing his recounting with, "It was that night that I
decided the two of us had to be friends."

She murmured some agreements and watched the
street for shadows. A sudden, chill wind cut through,
whipped around her shoulders. The raw hunger was
building inside her, desperate and undeniable. Rod
stopped walking. "I've been looking for a playmate,
Nidhi. I want you to be my playmate."

A shadow moved up the side of the building across
the street.

She started to reply, but her attention shifted to the
ambiguous shadow moving across the roof. They stopped
at the corner, and she noticed Rod also watching the
obscure mass gliding through the night.

"You have something to take care of." He ran his
hand down the sleeve of her bomber jacket. "We'll play

together another day." He jogged backward, calling his goodnight. Then spun and headed back the way they'd come.

The shadow too was gone.

Or at least hidden.

For now.

Nidhi took out her phone, mapped her way to the T.

Chapter Twelve
"I hear it didn't go as expected."

The subway car, one of the last of the night, held three other people, all clustered at the opposite end and all three deep in drunken conversation. Nidhi, still feeling the chill, slumped into a seat across from the door, stared at her reflection in the window. The car swayed along the tracks, lights flashing and fading as it cut across town. As Nidhi watched through the glass, a hand appeared on the other side, high up in the window.

Fingers outstretched, pale skin hard against the glass. The walls of the underground behind.

Her.

It.

Mattie.

The shadow on the building. The cold air cutting through her. The hunger deep in that black part of her heart.

The hand stayed on the glass, flattened and unmoving.

The train trundled on. The hand remained.

The wheels hummed, clattered, the car jerked. The hand remained.

Cages. Creatures. Cameras. Crowds.

Dirt. Destruction. Demands.

Historics by Hume.

153

Bansal Properties.

Bansal.

Mom and Dad.

Her mom and dad.

That section of town was known for its gentrification. The bookstore must have been one of the renovated buildings. Renovated by Elizabeth's husband. There was meaning in the connections, something Nidhi did not want to consider. Her mind chased the possibility away. Yet, it returned and remained as constant as the hand on the other side of the window.

Guy Belmont.

Rod McKinnon.

The hand.

Elizabeth Hume.

Hayden Thomas.

The hand.

Bansal Properties.

The hand.

Her.

It.

Mattie's hand.

Mom and Dad.

The car stopped at Boylston. Nidhi got out, not changing the pace of her stride when she emerged into the rain waiting for her on the street. She shivered but not from the rain. It was from the relentless chill now coming from within her own body, icing her spine, cooling her blood. The bitter taste in the back of her throat settled there, lingering like a threat.

This time, though, she didn't fight that warning. Resent it or dislike it.

She welcomed it. Accepted it.

All of it.

Even the shadow presence now trailing along behind her.

By the time she reached the Central Burying Ground, her soaked bomber jacket hung heavily on her shoulders, flat to her breasts. The wrought iron railing was slick, shining from the glow of the streetlamps. She went into the cemetery, stepping over the branches left from the storm.

Established on the Common in 1756, it was considered one of the most unique, cemeteries in the country. It's not popular with the picture-taking tourists but, due to its special history, is with the ghost hunters. In the early 1800's, the mayor appropriated a corner, took out a row of tombs. He ordered the construction of a platform, The Dell, and *relocated the remains*. Later, toward the end of 1800's, when the subway was being built, bodies of British soldiers who died during the occupation of the city were discovered in the area surrounding the cemetery. Bodies, unwanted and unwelcome, buried in unmarked graves. The city dumped them into a mass grave in the northwest edge. Nidhi knew all this because her parents told her. They'd told her a lot of such historic facts. Tidbits about the properties around town, snippets of history having to do with the buildings, the locations. All information related to *the properties*.

Now she gazed over the battered headstones. How many other nameless bodies had been left here? Bodies that had once been human, dumped into the ground, unmarked, unknown. Rotten and forgotten.

She smirked and moved deeper in, swiping at the rain dripping from her hair.

"Finding something funny, baby?"

"Come with me and find out."

Nidhi marched ahead. Mattie followed.

Overhead, the tree branches, now showing the tiniest buds of spring, dipped from the wind. Rain drops drizzled from trees and came down from the sky. The ground was flat, and except for the narrow dirt path, not much to look at. The Instagram warriors were right to spend their time in other, more picturesque burial grounds. Nidhi went to The Dell, hopped up on the raised platform, walking across the mass grave of nameless bodies. In the spring, when the trees had real leaves, and the cherry trees and magnolia bloomed, the lifeless ground would turn green with fresh grass and be respectable. But for now, it was battered, muddy from the rain, and a very ordinary brown.

"Is this your secret place?"

Mattie was beside her now, eyes glowing green. The soaked fabric of her skirt limp against her body. Her hair, hanging in clumps, dripping. Dots of water clinging to her eyelashes. Lips moist.

Nidhi moved to the middle of the long narrow area, spread her arms wide. "There are no secrets here, Mattie." Rain splattered her face, ran down the front of her neck, rolled under her bra. "No cameras to document your evil shit. No teas, oils, or ropes. No trees to hide behind. No people to watch." She tipped her head, eyeing the other girl over her shoulder. "Unless you count the passersby, trying to get home. But I don't think they care much about any impromptu sex show."

"You think that's what I care about?"

She unzipped her jacket, let the rain fall onto her t shirt. "I know it's what you care about."

Mattie set her hands on her hips, rolled her shoulders

back, let her leather fall open to reveal the red bindings covering her huge tits. "Haven't you realized?" she said, tucking her thumb under one of the bindings and pulling it down. "You don't know what you don't know."

"But I do... realize." Nidhi shrugged out of her jacket, tossed it to the wet ground.

Lights from the cars on Boylston zigzagged beyond, the cars sending hissing sprays of water into the air. A truck rumbled past, cornering so tightly the gush was visible through the trees.

Mattie pulled down another strap, revealed one well rounded breast. "Is that what you have in mind." She pinched her own nipple. "An impromptu sex show?"

Nidhi stared into Mattie's glimmering green eyes. "Looks to me like it's what you came for." She lifted her t shirt, tossed it on top of the jacket. "Take it off." Nidhi made a circle around Mattie. "Your jacket. Take it off."

Mattie did as she was told. Tossed the jacket down.

Nidhi came forward, grabbed at the bindings and pulled. The wet straps were twisted together, whipping away from Mattie's body as she tugged on each one. There were three in all, and she dropped them to the ground in a heavy, wet jumble. Rivulets of water rolled down from Mattie's shoulders, skittering across her breasts, trickled down her hard stomach. Nidhi lowered her mouth to one of the nipples and sucked, pulling it gently between her teeth until she felt it stiffened against her tongue. She grabbed the other breast, feeling the weight of it in her palm, flicking the nipple with her thumb, feeling cold satisfaction when that one too became hard, and Mattie's breath hitched.

"How long has it been since someone touched you?"

Mattie's hands were around her, her fingers working

on the strap of her bra. Nidhi reached back, unhooked it, tossed it to the ground and then embraced the other girl, savoring the explosion of carnal energy when Mattie's bare tits flattened against her own. She reached up, pulled Mattie's face to hers, pressed her rain-soaked lips to Mattie's. Their kiss started out tentative, each one exploring the edges of the other's mouth. The joining wasn't like the others. Their first moments had been performative, the prerequisite type done to impress the other. Then later, those were angry, cruel exchanges.

This joining was something else, something completely new and different.

Nidhi kept her hand on the back of Mattie's neck, holding their mouths together, deepening the kiss by dipping her tongue into Mattie's frosty mouth. They stayed in the embrace, locked together by their mouths, letting the rain roll down and over them. Finally, Nidhi lifted her head and eased back. The eerie gleam in Mattie's eyes, piercing now, shone through the rain. Nidhi took Mattie's hand, pulled her toward the edge of the platform. Once she reached the perimeter, she let go and jumped, landing on the flat area right in front of the low-sloped rise that rose up to the area dotted by tombstones.

She pulled off her boots. "Take it all off. I want to see you naked on the ground. I want to feel all your skin against mine."

Mattie leapt from the platform, began unlacing her boots. She yanked off her tattered tights, unhooked her skirt. Naked now, she sat on the ground, wrapped her arms around her calves, and stayed curled into herself.

Nidhi threw her jeans onto her boots and went to Mattie, knelt in front of her, put her palms on her knees.

"It's just us now." She pushed her knees apart, crawled between them and kissed Mattie again, stretching them both out to their full lengths, dripping warm body to dripping cold body, as she deepened the kiss.

Mattie's wrapped her arms around Nidhi's back, squeezed the two of them together so firmly they each to gasped for air.

"You think this is going to change anything, Nidhi? This sweet romance in the rain?" Using the weight of her body, she shifted them, turning them until she was on top. "You think we are going to be lovers? Run away together?" She planted her hands beside Nidhi shoulders, arching up and staring down with her unnatural green gaze. "Don't you remember what I told you about Matthew?"

"He isn't here, is he?" Nidhi tucked her arms inside Mattie's, pressed until Mattie crumpled on top of her. She took the other girl's head in her hands and the kiss continued, their mouths saying what words could not express. The pain of being alone, being used, being rejected, and ultimately, being betrayed by the ones you trusted, needed, the most. The black hole of the abyss was never ending and the two of them tumbled into it, together but still alone.

Nidhi rolled them again, this time pushing away and scrambling to get her mouth between Mattie's legs, taking control and giving the other girl what she wanted. What she needed to get through the night. Mattie's pussy was slick with rain and cold, so icy cold. But Nidhi slipped her tongue between the cool lips and found the small nub. She flicked it, licked it, and then took it into her mouth to suck and pull.

Mattie grabbed Nidhi's thighs and pushed her head between them, dipping down until she too found the tight,

159

hard nub between. The first bolt of electricity made Nidhi's spine snap but Mattie's grip on her legs was unrelenting. She continued the onslaught, using her tongue to thrust deeper in, licking the clit and then thrusting in, repeating the motions while her fingers pressed hard into the flesh of Nidhi's thighs. Fighting would do her no good. Resisting or pulling away, impossible. Taking the attack of pleasure, accepting her fate, were the only options her mind would allow. And so, she continued the attack of her own, sucking and flicking, over and over, her motions a message to Mattie to continue taking what she needed.

The first twinge of release came slowly, the tension building deep in her body, growing from an eerie place she had hidden from herself months ago. It was that place in her heart, that punishing spot, where the regrets grew and fed off one another. The release spread, her spine snapped again, this time getting stiff with murky tension and fear. Instinctively, she knew, the release was about to break something free. Let it out to roam her body and haunt her mind. She squirmed, trying to close her legs, to get Mattie's mouth from her body, but Mattie dug her hands deeper into the flesh, held tighter, so tight. Impossibly tight.

She arched back, gasped for air. She pawed at the dirt, her hands sliding each time she tried to get a grip and pull away. Over and over her hands glided across the mud, making two ruts. The coils of angry tension spun tighter and harder.

Tighter and harder.

And finally, Nidhi gave up.

The black force exploded inside her, shattering her will, breaking her. She hung in that empty space, teetering between nothing and everything, hanging there, waiting, not knowing on which side she would land. Loitering. Waiting. Until finally, she fell, landing resolutely on the side where she knew she belonged.

Without knowing or caring if Mattie had come as well, she gathered her jeans and other items on the slope, struggled to get them on. She climbed up onto the platform. Mattie, still naked, followed. When Mattie reached for her bindings, Nidhi snatched them away, taking them with her to where she'd left her shirt and jacket. She pulled the vial from the lining, held it out.

Mattie's leather dangled from her fist. "What is it?"

Nidhi stuffed the red straps into the lining of her jacket, held the vial out again. "Take it and find out."

Mattie dropped her leather then snatched the vial, twisted off the top, lifted it to her nose. "Where did you get this?"

Nidhi walked to the high edge of the platform, jumped, and started the walk to Acorn Street.

* * *

Nidhi waited under a gushing eave. The rain had started again about an hour ago. A cozy drizzle at first but had, in the last few moments, turned into a deluge. Guy Belmont was coming toward the building, a wide black umbrella over his head. The rainwater was pouring off the edges, making a circular waterfall effect. The old man splashed through the puddles with an unusual speed. She leaned into the door, holding it open long enough for him to slip inside.

He held the umbrella away from himself and shook it, sending droplets into the air. He straightened. It was after hours in the middle of the week, and, at the moment, the hallway was empty. "Right on time, Nidhi. And right where we belong."

She stayed put, watching as he finished closing the umbrella. He tapped the top point of it on the tile floor. After the last of the droplets fell, he held it toward her. She took it and wrapped the closure. Next, he unbuttoned his overcoat. The grey suit jacket beneath was pressed but probably done back about the time she was watching Dora the Explorer on VHS. He flattened the lapels, smoothed his bland grey paisley tie.

"I don't think you needed to get so dressed up."

"This is an important day. It is my return."

"About that…"

He reached inside his jacket. "Here."

Finally. The book was thinner than she expected. "The graphic design department went all out on this one," she said, tapping her finger against the cover, an abstract combination of lines and squares, all shades of grey.

"What were you expecting? A bodice ripper style featuring a woman tied to a tree?"

"Yeah. Good point."

"It will have everything you need and want." He pursed his lips and frowned. "And much that you do not need. Or want."

They started down the hall, their shoes thudding. "You nervous?" she asked, waiting for him to catch up.

He patted his jacket again and then flattened what was left of his lumpy hair. "Of course not."

She caught his gaze then lifted her eyebrows.

"Do not worry about me, Ms. Bansal. I'm finally, after all these years, about to start getting what I deserve. I have you to thank, so, thank you."

She lifted the book. "Fair trade," she said, then slipped the small tome into her messenger bag.

Her advisor, Professor Riviera, always left her door ajar, so Nidhi went straight to the doorway and let her know they'd arrived.

"Let's talk across the hall," the professor said from her desk. "Tremont is joining us."

Nidhi hadn't planned on dealing with the pain in the ass grad director. Even though the guy was old money Boston from way back, he still insisted on pretending he actually had to work for a living. Everyone knew he'd only gotten the job because his father-in-law was the president.

She pivoted, dodged Guy who was idling in the hall, and then went to the conference room. Tremont was already seated at the round table, looking his part in his brown tweed jacket.

"Hello, Trenton. That's really nice of you to join us, but—" She started to introduce Guy, but Trenton had already rushed to his feet and outstretched his hand.

The two went through their greeting without her. Guy took the seat beside the grad director. By the time Nidhi had taken off her coat and sat, Professor Riviera had already taken a seat across from Trenton and started the conversation. The rapid-fire exchanges were minimal and concluded with her advisor assuring Nidhi the dissertation proposal was approved. Her work on cults recruiting from fandoms could move forward without the proposal defense.

"And so, Trenton and I have already signed your candidacy form. Mr. Belmont, would you—"

" *Professor* Belmont."

"Yes, yes of course." She slid the form across the

table and topped it with a pen. "Professor Belmont, would you please sign Ms. Bansal's form?"

"I look forward to being on her committee, so I am happy to sign the form in support of her very compelling project."

As soon as Guy lifted the pen, Professor Riviera whisked the paper away and stood. "I'll take care of the rest, Nidhi. Thank you again *Professor* Belmont."

"I haven't done anything yet," he said. "I do, however, plan—"

"Yes, of course you have plans," Trenton was on his feet too, smoothing back his waxed hair. "We are glad to hear that and look forward to working with you."

Guy pushed himself up. "Thank you both. I'm looking forward to it as well."

Nidhi's heart pounded as she too got to her feet. "You don't have any questions for Mr. Belmont?"

Trenton moved toward the door. "No, *Professor* Belmont's work speaks for itself."

Guy offered his appreciation again then hustled himself, old man style, out of the room.

Nidhi mumbled her thanks as well, slipped on her coat, and moved toward the door.

Trenton stopped her by calling her name. When she turned back, he said, "Be sure to thank your parents for us."

Nidhi set her palm on the doorframe. "Thank… them?"

"For the very generous donation."

"Trenton!" Then to Nidhi, Professor Riviera said, "They requested that their donation remain anonymous. You know how they are… so, please, don't mention it."

No, she had not known how they were.

But she was just now beginning to figure it out.

* * *

Nidhi was seated on the brocade sofa when Hayden, texted to ask if he could stop by. The rest of the glass vials, the leather notebook with the red band, and the key were on the coffee table. This time, she didn't hide them. And, after he sat on the couch, she sat beside him, not caring that their thighs were pressed together.

"Where did you get that?" he asked, gesturing to the stash.

"Rod McKinon, I think."

Hayden let out a sigh. "Those herbs look like him. I don't know about the key. What's the journal."

She handed it to him.

He flipped through. "You know what this back part is, right?"

"Yeah." A recording of the auctions. A code indicating who bought what. Or rather who bought whom. How much they paid, that was easy, a number. When, a date. Also, easy to understand. What happened after, no record of that.

Who bought them? Someone who had access and also a shit ton of money.

Hayden flipped through it again, stopped on the last page. The journal ended a year ago, before either of them were involved.

"What's the key for?"

"Don't know." She got up and pulled back the fireplace flue. "In all the time I've lived here, I've never once used the fireplace."

He picked the key up, pinched it between his fingers. "I'm thinking I need to start living this lifestyle."

Hayden watched her tuck a fire starter pack under

each of the dusty logs. "Pretty standard key." He said. "Not old."

The matches were in a small pouch hanging with the bespoke tool kit. She struck one, lit the edge of one pack. "Yeah, just opens the door to some building. Some building that…"

"What's a building that Rod, or whoever, would know matters?"

She struck another match, lit another pack.

"There's one place I know of, but one key won't get you in there." He set the key on the table with a faint clink.

She went back to the sofa, took the spot next to him again.

"I turned in the list. I thought you should know." He let the words hang as he eased back into the cushions, watched the small flames, creep out of the packs, hit the edges of the logs.

"My parents told me that oak is hard to get started. Like it resists being burned."

"I've heard that too." Hayden set one foot on the edge of the coffee table then crossed the other over it. He closed his eyes. "Do you want to see the list I turned in to Elizabeth? I saved you a copy, in case…"

"They said that once the flames get going, the fire is intense and burns for a long, long time."

"I didn't know that." He opened one eye. "Do you want to see the list?"

"No." She watched the flames spread, already being to feed off the wood. "I already know what it'll tell me."

* * *

A Taco Bell bag flew across the sidewalk in front of The Southie, flipping and twisting in the damp night wind. It collided with a lamppost and hung there, the edges shaking, the center flattened. Across the street, weed smoke and country music drifted out of an open window. The nail salon was dark. The closed sign hung sideways, seeming to point down to the welcome mat on the other side of the door. Inside the building in front of her there was no sign of life, but that was fine. It wasn't life she was interested in. The key fit, the door opened.

Nidhi closed it behind her, locked it, then crossed over the battered linoleum, kicking two pink cups out of her way. A stack of pink cups was on the bar, a half full pitcher beside it. She filled one of the cups and took it with her to the door in battered the back. The muffled rumble of industrial cyberpunk came through the old wood.

She took a swallow, winced, banged her fist on the door, hard enough to make the locks on the other side bounce.

Waited.

She banged again. Took another sip.

Waited again. For the liquid to take effect and for the door to swing open.

Banged again. Downed the rest.

She listened to soft metallic clink of the locks being moved on the other side and then waited. The door bounced against the wall. One of the locks fell to the stairs, tumbling down three risers.

Matthew's head was angled up, his gaze on Nidhi's breasts, now bound with the red bands.

Nidhi dropped the empty cup, kicked it to the side.

Matthew turned, went down.

Nidhi replaced the locks, clicking each of the three into

place. And then she went down. She stopped at the bottom, looked left. Looked right.
She walked straight ahead.

About the Author

Isabelle Drake got her start writing confession stories for pulp magazines like *True Confessions* and *True Love*. Since publishing those first few stories she has written in multiple genres, earned an MFA in Creative Writing and become an English & Writing Professor.

When away from her keyboard, she watches films, especially classic noir, horror and romance, and reads (of course). An avid traveler, she'll go just about anywhere—at least once—to meet people and get ideas.

Find Isabelle Drake on Facebook, Instagram and all the social as @isabelledrake.

Other Riverdale Avenue Books You Might Enjoy

Mistress of the Undead
By Isabelle Drake

Servant of the Undead
By Isabelle Drake

Rabid Heart
By Jeremy Wagner

The Armageddon Chord
By Jeremy Wagner

A Tribute Anthology to
Deadworld and Comic Publisher Gary Reed
Edited by Lori Perkins

Still Hungry for Your Love
Edited by Lori Perkins

Women Who Love Monsters
Edited by Lori Perkins

The Morris-Jumel Mansion
Anthology of Paranormal Fiction
Edited by Camilla Saly-Monzingo